Books are on loan for 21 days from date of issue.

Fines for overdue books: 10p for each week or portion
of a week plus cost of postage incurred in recovery.

D1348310

HEINEMANN
NEW WINDMILLS

THE BEST OF
BERNARD MAC LAVERTY

Why won't Neil swim in the sea even at the expense of losing his friendship with Michael? What does Nelson learn about his mother when he plays truant from school? Can a father and son overcome the great emotional gulf between them and talk to each other?

Bernard Mac Laverty's short stories explore some of the deeply embarrassing and painful moments of our lives and offer us humorous and poignant insights into the ways we think and feel.

ABOUT THE AUTHOR

Bernard Mac Laverty was born in Belfast and lived there until he was in his early thirties. He has been a medical laboratory technician, a mature student, a teacher and for two years the Writer-in-Residence at Aberdeen University. He is now a full-time writer and lives in Glasgow.

He has published three collections of short stories: *Secrets, A Time to Dance* and *The Great Profundo* and two novels: *Lamb* and *Cal*. He has also written radio, television and screen plays.

Cal is also published in the New Windmill Series.

The Best of
BERNARD MAC LAVERTY
SHORT STORIES

HEINEMANN
NEW WINDMILLS

Heinemann Educational Publishers
Halley Court, Jordan Hill, Oxford OX2 8EJ
a division of Reed Educational & Professional Publishing Ltd
OXFORD   MELBOURNE   AUCKLAND
JOHANNESBURG   BLANTYRE   GABORONE
IBADAN   PORTSMOUTH (NH) USA   CHICAGO

ISBN 0 435 12365 3

This collection first published in the New Windmill Series in
1990
98 99 11 10 9 8 7

Bernard Mac Laverty's short stories were first published in the
following volumes:

Secrets and Other Stories. Blackstaff Press Ltd 1977
The Exercise
The Miraculous Candidate
A Rate and Some Renovations
Secrets
Where the Tides Meet
The Deep End
Copyright © 1977 by Bernard Mac Laverty

A Time to Dance. Jonathan Cape 1982
Father and Son
A Time to Dance
My Dear Palestrina
The Beginnings of a Sin
Copyright © 1982 by Bernard Mac Laverty

The Great Profundo and Other Stories. Jonathan Cape Ltd 1987
More than Just the Disease
Copyright © 1987 by Bernard Mac Laverty

The stories appeared previously, as listed: 'The Beginnings of a Sin'
(In Dublin, 1981). 'Father and Son' (Scottish Short Stories, Collins,
1987), 'My Dear Palestrina' (BBC Radio 4, 1980; BBC Television,
1980); 'A Time to Dance' (Scottish Short Stories, Collins, 1980)

Cover illustration by Peter Melnycznk

Printed in England by Clays Ltd, St Ives plc

J96, 839
6. 25

Contents

The Exercise

'We never got the chance,' his mother would say to him. 'It wouldn't have done me much good but your father could have bettered himself. He'd be teaching or something now instead of serving behind a bar. He could stand up with the best of them.'

Now that he had started grammar school Kevin's father joined him in his work, helping him when he had the time, sometimes doing the exercises out of the text books on his own before he went to bed. He worked mainly from examples in the Maths and Language books or from previously corrected work of Kevin's. Often his wife took a hand out of him, saying 'Do you think you'll pass your Christmas Tests?'

When he concentrated he sat hunched at the kitchen table, his non-writing hand shoved down the back of his trousers and his tongue stuck out.

'Put that thing back in your mouth,' Kevin's mother would say, laughing. 'You've a tongue on you like a cow.'

His father smelt strongly of tobacco for he smoked both a pipe and cigarettes. When he gave Kevin money for sweets he'd say, 'You'll get sixpence in my coat pocket on the bannisters.'

Kevin would dig into the pocket deep down almost to his elbow and pull out a handful of coins speckled with bits of yellow and black tobacco. His father also smelt of porter, not his breath, for he never drank but from his clothes and Kevin thought it mixed nicely with his grown up smell. He loved to smell his pyjama jacket and the shirts that he left off for washing.

1

Once in a while Kevin's father would come in at six o'clock, sit in his armchair and say, 'Slippers'.

'You're not staying in, are you? The three boys shouted and danced around, the youngest pulling off his big boots, falling back on the floor as they came away from his feet, Kevin, the eldest, standing on the arm of the chair to get the slippers down from the cupboard.

'Some one of you get a good shovel of coal for that fire,' and they sat in the warm kitchen doing their homework, their father reading the paper or moving about doing some job that their mother had been at him to do for months. Before their bedtime he would read the younger ones a story or if there were no books in the house at the time he would choose a piece from the paper. Kevin listened with the others although he pretended to be doing something else.

But it was not one of those nights. His father stood shaving with his overcoat on, a very heavy navy overcoat, in a great hurry, his face creamed thick with white lather. Kevin knelt on the cold lino of the bathroom floor, one elbow leaning on the padded seat of the green wicker chair trying to get help with his Latin. It was one of those exercises which asked for the nominative and genitive of: an evil deed, a wise father and so on.

'What's the Latin for "evil"?'

His father towered above him trying to get at the mirror, pointing his chin upwards scraping underneath.

'Look it up at the back.'

Kevin sucked the end of his pencil and fumbled through the vocabularies. His father finished shaving, humped his back and spluttered in the basin. Kevin heard him pull the plug and the final gasp as the water escaped. He groped for the towel then genuflected beside him drying his face.

'Where is it?' He looked down still drying slower and slower, meditatively until he stopped.

'I'll tell you just this once because I'm in a hurry.'

Kevin stopped sucking the pencil and held it poised, ready and wrote the answers with great speed into his jotter as his father called them out.

'Is that them all?' his father asked, draping the towel over the side of the bath. He leaned forward to kiss Kevin but he lowered his head to look at something in the book. As he rushed down the stairs he shouted back over his shoulder.

'Don't ever ask me to do that again. You'll have to work them out for yourself.'

He was away leaving Kevin sitting at the chair. The towel edged its way slowly down the side of the bath and fell on the floor. He got up and looked in the wash-hand basin. The bottom was covered in short black hairs, shavings. He drew a white path through them with his finger. Then he turned and went down the stairs to copy the answers in ink.

Of all the teachers in the school Waldo was the one who commanded the most respect. In his presence nobody talked, with the result that he walked the corridors in a moat of silence. Boys seeing him approach would drop their voices to a whisper and only when he was out of earshot would they speak normally again. Between classes there was always five minutes uproar. The boys wrestled over desks, shouted, whistled, flung books while some tried to learn their nouns, eyes closed, feet tapping to the rhythm of declensions. Others put frantic finishing touches to last night's exercise. Some minutes before Waldo's punctual arrival, the class quietened. Three rows of boys, all by now strumming nouns, sat hunched and waiting.

Waldo's entrance was theatrical. He strode in with strides as long as his soutane would permit, his books clenched in his left hand and pressed tightly against his chest. With his right hand he swung the door behind him, closing it with a crash. His eyes raked the class. If, as occasionally happened, it did not close properly he did not turn from the class but backed slowly against the door snapping it shut with his behind. Two strides brought him to the rostrum. He cracked his books down with an explosion and made a swift palm upward gesture.

Waldo was very tall, his height being emphasised by the soutane, narrow and tight-fitting at the shoulders, sweeping down like a bell to the floor. A row of black gleaming buttons bisected him from the floor to throat. When he talked his Adam's apple hit against the hard, white Roman collar and created in Kevin the same sensation as a fingernail scraping down the blackboard. His face was sallow and immobile. (There was a rumour that he had a glass eye but no-one knew which. Nobody could look at him long enough because to meet his stare was to invite a question.) He abhorred slovenliness. Once when presented with an untidy exercise book, dog-eared with a tea ring on the cover, he picked it up, the corner of one leaf between his finger and thumb, the pages splaying out like a fan, opened the window and dropped it three floors to the ground. His own neatness became exaggerated when he was at the board, writing in copperplate script just large enough for the boy in the back row to read — geometrical columns of declined nouns defined by exact, invisible margins. When he had finished he would set the chalk down and rub the used finger and thumb together with the same action he used after handling the host over the paten.

The palm upward gesture brought the class to its feet and they said the Hail Mary in Latin. While it was being said all eyes looked down because they knew if they looked up Waldo was bound to be staring at them.

'Exercises.'

When Waldo was in a hurry he corrected the exercises verbally, asking one boy for the answers and then asking all those who got it right to put up their hands. It was four for anyone who lied about his answer and now and then he would take spot checks to find out the liars.

'Hold it, hold it there,' he would say and leap from the rostrum, moving through the forest of hands and look at each boy's book, tracing out the answer with the tip of his cane. Before the end of the round and while his attention was on one book a few hands would be lowered quietly. Today he was in a hurry. The atmosphere was tense as he looked from one boy to another, deciding who would start.

'Sweeny, we'll begin with you.' Kevin rose to his feet, his finger trembling under the place in the book. He read the first answer and looked up at Waldo. He remained impassive. He would let someone while translating unseens ramble on and on with great imagination until he faltered, stopped and admitted that he didn't know. Then and only then would he be slapped.

'Two, nominative. *Sapienter Pater.*' Kevin went on haltingly through the whole ten and stopped, waiting for a comment from Waldo. It was a long time before he spoke. When he did it was with bored annoyance.

'Every last one of them is wrong.'

'But sir, Father, they couldn't be wr. . .' Kevin said it with such conviction, blurted it out so quickly that Waldo looked at him in surprise.

'Why not?'

'Because my. . .' Kevin stopped.

'Well?' Waldo's stone face resting on his knuckles. 'Because my what?'

It was too late to turn back now.

'Because my father said so,' he mumbled very low, chin on chest.

'Speak up, let us all hear you.' Some of the boys had heard and he thought they sniggered.

'Because my father said so.' This time the commotion in the class was obvious.

'And where does your father teach Latin?' There was no escape. Waldo had him. He knew now there would be an exhibition for the class. Kevin placed his weight on his arm and felt his tremble communicated to the desk.

'He doesn't, Father.'

'And what does he do?'

'He's a barman.'

'A barman!' Waldo mimicked and the class roared loudly.

'*Quiet.*' He wheeled on them. 'You Sweeny. Come out here.' He reached inside the breast of his soutane and with a flourish produced a thin yellow cane, whipping it back and forth, testing it.

Kevin walked out to the front of the class, his face fiery red, the blood throbbing in his ears. He held out his hand. Waldo raised it higher, more to his liking, with the tip of the cane touching the underside of the upturned palm. He held it there for some time.

'If your brilliant father continues to do your homework for you, Sweeny, you'll end up a barman yourself.' Then

5

he whipped the cane down expertly across the tips of his fingers and again just as the blood began to surge back into them. Each time the cane in its follow-through cracked loudly against the skirts of his soutane.

'You could have made a better job of it yourself. Other hand.' The same ritual of raising and lowering the left hand with the tip of the cane to the desired height. 'After all, I have taught you some Latin.' *Crack*. 'It would be hard to do any worse.'

Kevin went back to his place resisting a desire to hug his hands under his armpits and stumbled on a schoolbag jutting into the aisle as he pushed into his desk. Again Waldo looked round the class and said, 'Now we'll have it *right* from someone.'

The class continued and Kevin nursed his fingers, out of the fray.

As the bell rang Waldo gathered up his books and said, 'Sweeny, I want a word with you outside. Ave Maria, gratia plena. . .' It was not until the end of the corridor that Waldo turned to face him. He looked at Kevin and maintained his silence for a moment.

'Sweeny, I must apologise to you.' Kevin bowed his head. 'I meant your father no harm — he's probably a good man, a very good man.'

'Yes, sir,' said Kevin. The pain in his fingers had gone.

'Look at me when I'm talking, please.' Kevin looked at his collar, his Adam's apple, then his face. It relaxed for a fraction and Kevin thought he was almost going to smile, but he became efficient, abrupt again.

'All right, very good, you may go back to your class.'

'Yes Father,' Kevin nodded and moved back along the empty corridor.

Some nights when he had finished his homework early he would go down to meet his father coming from work. It was dark, October, and he stood close against the high wall at the bus-stop trying to shelter from the cutting wind. His thin black blazer with the school emblem on the breast pocket and his short grey trousers, both new for starting grammar school, did little to keep him warm. He stood shivering, his hands in his trouser pockets and looked down at his knees which were blue and marbled, quivering uncontrollably. It was six o'clock when he left the house and he had been standing for fifteen minutes. Traffic began to thin out and the buses became less regular, carrying fewer and fewer passengers. There was a moment of silence when there was no traffic and he heard a piece of paper scraping along on pointed edges. He kicked it as it passed him. He thought of what had happened, of Waldo and his father. On the first day in class Waldo had picked out many boys by their names.

'Yes, I know your father well,' or 'I taught your elder brother. A fine priest he's made. Next.'

'Sweeny, Father.'

'Sweeny? Sweeny? — You're not Dr John's son, are you?'

'No Father.'

'Or anything to do with the milk people?'

'No Father.'

'Next.' He passed on without further comment.

Twenty-five past six. Another bus turned the corner and Kevin saw his father standing on the platform. He moved forward to the stop as the bus slowed down. His father jumped lightly off and saw Kevin waiting for him. He clipped him over the head with the tightly rolled newspaper he was carrying.

'How are you big lad?'

'All right,' said Kevin shivering. He humped his shoulders and set off beside his father, bumping into him uncertainly as he walked.

'How did it go today?' his father asked.

'All right.' They kept silent until they reached the corner of their own street.

'What about the Latin?'

Kevin faltered, feeling a babyish desire to cry.

'How was it?'

'OK. Fine.'

'Good. I was a bit worried about it. It was done in a bit of a rush. Son, your Da's a genius.' He smacked him with the paper again. Kevin laughed and slipped his hand into the warmth of his father's overcoat pocket, deep to the elbow.

7

More than Just the Disease

As he unpacked his case Neil kept hearing his mother's voice. *Be tidy at all times, then no one can surprise you.* This was a strange house he'd come to, set in the middle of a steep terraced garden. Everything in it seemed of an unusual design; the wardrobe in which he hung his good jacket was of black lacquer with a yellow inlay of exotic birds. *A little too ornate for my taste — vulgar almost.* And pictures — there were pictures hanging everywhere, portraits, landscapes, sketches. *Dust gatherers.* The last things in his case were some comics and he laid them with his ironed and folded pyjamas on the pillow of the bottom bunk and went to join the others.

They were all sitting in the growing dark of the large front room, Michael drinking hot chocolate, Anne his sister with her legs flopped over the arm of the chair, Dr Middleton squeaking slowly back and forth in the rocking-chair while his wife moved around preparing to go out.

'Now, boys, you must be in bed by ten thirty at the latest. Anne can sit up until we come back if she wants. We'll not be far away and if anything does happen you can phone "The Seaview".' She spent some time looking in an ornamental jug for a pen to write down the number. 'I can find nothing in this house yet.'

'We don't need Anne to babysit,' said Michael. 'We're perfectly capable of looking after ourselves. Isn't that right Neil?' Neil nodded. He didn't like Michael involving him in an argument with the rest of the family. He had to have the tact of a guest; sit on the fence yet remain Michael's friend.

'Can we not stay up as late as Anne?' asked Michael.

'Anne is fifteen years of age. Please, Michael, it's been a long day. Off to bed.'

'But Mama, Neil and I. . .'

'Michael.' The voice came from the darkness of the rockingchair and had enough threat in it to stop Michael. The two boys got up and went to their bedroom.

Neil lifted his pyjamas and went to the bathroom. He dressed for bed buttoning the jacket right up to his neck and went back with his clothes draped over his arm. Michael was half-dressed.

'That was quick,' he said. He bent his thin arms, flexing his biceps. 'I only wear pyjama bottoms. Steve McQueen, he-man,' and he thumped his chest before climbing to the top bunk. They lay and talked and talked — about their first year at the school, how lucky they had been to have been put in the same form, who they hated most. The Crow with his black gown and beaky nose, the Moon with his pallid round face, wee Hamish with his almost mad preoccupation with ruling red lines. Once Neil had awkwardly ruled a line which showed the two bumps of his fingers protruding beyond the ruler and wee Hamish had pounced on it.

'What are these bumps? Is this a drawing of a camel, boy?' Everybody except Neil had laughed and if there was one thing he couldn't abide it was to be laughed at. A voice whispered that it was a drawing of his girlfriend's chest.

Neil talked about the Scholarship examination and the day he got his results. When he saw the fat envelope on the mat he knew his life would change — if you got the thin envelope you had failed, a fat one with coloured forms meant that you had passed. What Neil did not say was that his mother had cried, kneeling in the hallway hugging and kissing him. He had never seen anyone cry with happiness before and it worried him a bit. Nor did he repeat what she had said with her eyes shining. *Now you'll be at school with the sons of doctors and lawyers.*

Anne opened the door and hissed into the dark.

'You've got to stop talking right now. Get to sleep.' She was in a cotton nightdress which became almost transparent with the light of the hallway behind her. Neil saw her curved shape outlined to its margins. He wanted her to stay there but she slammed the door.

After that they whispered and had a farting competition. They heard Michael's father and mother come in, make tea and go to bed. It was ages before either of them slept. All the time Neil was in agonies with his itch but he did not want to scratch in case Michael should feel the shaking communicated to the top bunk.

In the morning Neil was first awake and tiptoed to the bathroom with all his clothes to get dressed. He took off his pyjama jacket and looked at himself in the mirror. Every morning he hoped that it would have miraculously disappeared overnight but it was still there crawling all over his chest and shoulders: his psoriasis — a redness with an edge as irregular as a map and the skin flaking and scumming off the top. Its pattern changed from week to week but only once had it appeared above his collar line. That week his mother had kept him off school. He turned his back on the mirror and put on a shirt, buttoning it up to the neck. He wondered if he should wear a tie to breakfast but his mother's voice had nothing to say on the subject.

Breakfast wasn't a meal like in his own house when he and his mother sat down at table and had cereal and tea and toast with sometimes a boiled egg. Here people just arrived and poured themselves cornflakes and went off to various parts of the room, or even the house, to eat them. The only still figure was the doctor himself. He sat at the corner of the table reading the *Scotsman* and drinking coffee. He wore blue running shoes and no socks and had a T-shirt on. Except for his receding M-shaped hairline he did not look at all like a doctor. In Edinburgh anytime Neil had seen him he wore a dark suit and a spotted bow-tie.

Anne came in. '*Guten Morgen, mein Papa.* Hello Neil.' She was bright and washed with her yellow hair in a knot on the top of her head. Neil thought she was the most beautiful girl he had ever seen up close. She wore a pair of denims cut down to shorts so that there were frayed fringes about her thighs. She also had what his mother called *a figure*. She ate her cornflakes noisily and the doctor did not even raise his eyes from the paper. *Close*

10

your mouth when you're eating, please. Others have to live with you.

'Some performance last night, eh Neil? she said.

'Pardon?'

'Daddy, they talked till all hours.'

Her father turned a page of the paper and his hand groped out like a blind man's to find his coffee.

'Sorry,' said Neil.

'I'm only joking,' said Anne and smiled at him. He blushed because she looked directly into his eyes and smiled at him as if she liked him. He stumbled to his feet.

'Thank you for the breakfast,' he said to the room in general and went outside to the garden where Michael was sitting on the steps.

'Where did you get to? You didn't even excuse yourself from the table,' said Neil.

'I wasn't at the table, small Fry,' said Michael. He was throwing pea-sized stones into an ornamental pond at a lower level.

'One minute you were there and the next you were gone.'

'I thought it was going to get heavy.'

'What?'

'I know the signs. The way the old man reads the paper. Coming in late last night.'

'Oh.'

Neil lifted a handful of multi-coloured gravel and fed the pieces singly into his other hand and lobbed them at the pool. They made a nice plip noise.

'Watch it,' said Michael. He stilled Neil's throwing arm with his hand. 'Here comes Mrs Wan.'

'Who's she?'

An old woman in a bottle-green cardigan and baggy mouse-coloured trousers came stepping one step at a time down towards them. She wore a puce-coloured hat like a turban and, although it was high summer, a pair of men's leather gloves.

'Good morning, boys,' she said. Her voice was the most superior thing Neil had ever heard, even more so than his elocution teacher's. 'And how are you this year, Benjamin?'

'Fine. This is my friend Neil Fry.' Neil stood up and nodded. She was holding secateurs and a flat wooden basket. He knew that she would find it awkward to shake hands so he did not offer his.

'How do you do? What do you think of my garden, young man?'

'It's very good. Tidy.'

'Let's hope it remains that way throughout your stay,' she said and continued her sideways stepping down until she reached the compost heap at the bottom beyond the ornamental pool.

'Who is she?' asked Neil.

'She owns the house. Lets it to us for the whole of the summer.'

'But where does she live when you're here?'

'Up the back in a caravan. She's got ninety million cats.' Mrs Wan's puce turban threaded in and out of the flowers as she weeded and pruned. It was a dull overcast day and the wind was moving the brightly-coloured rose blooms.

'Fancy a swim?' asked Michael.

'Too cold. Anyway I told you I can't swim.'

'You don't have to swim. Just horse around. It's great.'

'Naw.'

Michael threw his whole handful of gravel chippings into the pond and went up the steps to the house.

That afternoon the shelf of cloud moved inland and the sky over the Atlantic became blue. The wind dropped and Dr Middleton observed that the mare's-tails were a good sign. The whole family went down the hundred yards to the beach, each one carrying something — a basket, a deckchair, a lilo.

'Where else in the world but Scotland would we have the beach to ourselves on a day like this?' said Mrs Middleton. The doctor agreed with a grunt. Michael got stripped to his swimming trunks and they taught Neil to play boule in the hard sand near the water. The balls were of bright grooved steel and he enjoyed trying to lob them different ways until he finally copied the doctor who showed him how to put back-spin on them. Anne wore a turquoise bikini and kept

12

hooking her fingers beneath the elastic of her pants and snapping them out to cover more of her bottom. She did this every time she bent to pick up her boule and Neil came to watch for it. When they stopped playing Michael and his sister ran off to leap about in the breakers — large curling walls, glass-green, which nearly knocked them off their feet. From where he stood Neil could only hear their cries faintly. He went and sat down with the doctor and his wife.

'Do you not like the water?' she asked. She was lying on a sunbed, gleaming with suntan oil. She had her dress rucked up beyond her knees and her shoulder straps loosened.

'No. It's too cold.'

'The only place *I'll* ever swim again is the Med,' said the doctor.

'Sissy', said his wife, without opening her eyes. Neil lay down and tried to think of a better reason for not swimming. His mother had one friend who occasionally phoned for her to go to the Commonwealth Pool. When she really didn't feel like it there was only one excuse that seemed to work.

At tea Michael took a perverse pleasure out of telling him again and again how warm the water was and Anne innocently agreed with him.

The next day was scorching hot. Even at breakfast time they could see the heat corrugating the air above the slabbed part of the garden.

'You *must* come in for a swim today, Fry. I'm boiled already,' said Michael.

'The forecast is twenty-one degrees,' said the doctor from behind his paper. Anne whistled in appreciation.

Neil's thighs were sticking to the plastic of his chair. He said, 'My mother forgot to pack my swimming trunks. I looked yesterday.'

Mrs Middleton, in a flowing orange dressing-gown, spoke over her shoulder from the sink. 'Borrow a pair of Michael's.' Before he could stop her she had gone off with wet hands in search of extra swimming trunks.

'Couldn't be simpler,' she said, setting a navy blue pair with white side panels on the table in front of Neil.

13

'I'll get mine,' said Michael and dashed to his room. Anne sat opposite Neil on the Formica kitchen bench-top swinging her legs. She coaxed him to come swimming, again looking into his eyes. He looked down and away from them.

'Come on, Neil. Michael's not much fun in the water.'

'The fact is,' said Neil, 'I've got my period.'

There was a long silence and a slight rustle of the *Scotsman* as Dr Middleton looked over the top of it. Then Anne half-slid, half-vaulted off the bench and ran out. Neil heard her make funny snorts in her nose.

'That's too bad,' said the doctor and got up and went out of the room shutting the door behind him. Neil heard Anne's voice and her father's, then he heard the bedroom door shut. He folded his swimming trunks and set them on the sideboard. Mrs Middleton gave a series of little coughs and smiled at him.

'Can I help you with the dishes?' he asked. There was something not right.

'Are you sure you're well enough?' she said smiling. Neil nodded and began to lift the cups from various places in the room. She washed and he dried with a slow thoroughness.

'Neil, nobody is going to force you to swim. So you can feel quite safe.'

Michael came in with his swimming gear in a roll under his arm.

'Ready, small Fry?'

'Michael, could I have a word? Neil, could you leave those bathing trunks back in Michael's wardrobe?'

On the beach the boys lay down on the sand. Michael hadn't spoken since they left the house. He walked in front, he picked the spot, he lay down and Neil followed him. The sun was hot and again they had the beach to themselves. Neil picked up a handful of sand and examined it as he spilled it out slowly.

'I bet you there's at least one speck of gold on this beach,' he said.

'That's a bloody stupid thing to say.'

'I'll bet you there is.'

Michael rolled over turning his back. 'I can pick them.'

'What?'

'I can really pick them.'

'What do you mean?'

'I might as well have asked a girl to come away on holiday.' Neil's fist bunched in the sand.

'What's the use of somebody who won't go in for a dip?'

'I can't, that's all.'

'My Mum says you must have a very special reason. What is it, Fry?'

Neil opened his hand and some of the damp, deeper sand remained in little segments where he had clenched it. He was almost sure Anne had laughed.

'I'm not telling you.'

'Useless bloody Mama's boy,' said Michael. He got up flinging a handful of sand at Neil and ran down to the water. Some of the sand went into Neils's eyes, making him cry. He knuckled them clear and blinked, watching Michael jump, his elbows up, as each glass wave rolled at him belly-high.

Neil shouted hopelessly towards the sea. 'That's the last time I'm getting you into the pictures.'

He walked back towards the house. He had been here a night, a day and a morning. It would be a whole week before he could get home. Right now he felt he *was* a Mama's boy. He just wanted to climb the stair and be with her behind the closed door of their house. This had been the first time in his life he had been away from her and, although he had been reluctant because of this very thing, she had insisted that he could not turn down an invitation from the doctor's family. *It will teach you how to conduct yourself in good society.*

At lunch time Michael did not speak to him but made up salad rolls and took them on to the patio. Anne and her father had gone into the village on bicycles. Neil sat at the table chewing his roll with difficulty and staring in front of him. *If there is one thing I cannot abide it's a milk bottle on the table.* Mrs Middleton was the only one left for him to talk to.

'We met Mrs Wan this morning,' he said.

'Oh did you? She's a rum bird — feeding all those cats.'

15

'How many has she?'

'I don't know. They're never all together at the same time. She's a Duchess, you know?'

'A real one?'

'Yes. I can't remember her title — from somewhere in England. She married some Oriental and lived in the Far East. Africa too for a time. When he died she came home. Look.' She waved her hand at all the bric-à-brac. 'Look at this.' She went to a glass-fronted cabinet and took out what looked like a lace ball. It was made of ivory and inside was another ball with just as intricately carved mandarins and elephants and palm leaves, with another one inside that again.

'The question is how did they carve the one inside. It's all one piece.'

Neil turned it over in his hands marvelling at the mystery. He handed it carefully back

'You wouldn't want to play boule with that,' he said.

'Isn't it exquisitely delicate?'

He nodded and said, 'Thank you for the lunch. It was very nourishing.'

He wandered outside in the garden and sat for a while by the pool. It was hot and the air was full of the noise of insects and bees moving in and out the flowers. He went down to the beach and saw that his friend Michael had joined up with some other boys to play cricket. He sat down out of sight of them at the side of a sand-dune. He lay back and closed his eyes. They had laughed at him in school when he said he didn't know what l.b.w. meant. He had been given a free cricket bat but there was hardly a mark on it because he couldn't seem to hit the ball. It was so hard and came at him so fast that he was more interested in getting out of its way than playing any fancy strokes. Scholarship boys were officially known as foundationers but the boys called them 'fundies' or 'fundaments'. When he asked what it meant somebody told him to look it up in a dictionary. 'Part of body on which one sits; buttocks; anus.'

He lifted his head and listened. At first he thought it was the noise of a distant seagull but it came again and he knew it wasn't. He looked up to the top of the sand-dune and saw a kitten, its tiny black tail upright and quivering.

'Pshhh-wshhh.'

He climbed the sand and lifted it. It miaowed thinly. He stroked its head and back and felt the frail fish bones of its ribs. It purred and he carried it back to the house. He climbed the steps behind the kitchen and saw a caravan screened by a thick hedge. The door was open and he had to hold it steady with his knee before he could knock on it.

'Come in,' Mrs Wan's voice called. Neil stepped up into the van. After the bright sunlight it was gloomy inside. It smelt of old and cat. He saw Mrs Wan sitting along one wall with her feet up.

'I found this and thought maybe it was yours,' said Neil handing the cat over to her. She scolded it.

'You little monkey,' she said and smiled at Neil. 'This cat is a black sheep. He's always wandering off. Thank you, young man. It was very kind of you to take the trouble to return him.'

'It was no trouble.'

She was dressed as she had been the day before except for the gloves. Her hands were old and her fingers bristled with rings. She waved at him as he turned to go.

'Just a minute. Would you like something to drink — as a reward?' She stood up and rattled in a cupboard above the sink.

'I think some tonic water is all I can offer you. Will that do?' She didn't give him a clean glass but just rinsed one for a moment under the thin trickle from the swan-neck tap at the tiny sink. She chased three cats away from the covered bench and waved him to sit down. Because the glass was not very clean the bubbles adhered to its sides. He saw that nothing was clean as he looked about the place. There were several tins of Kit-e-Kat opened on the draining-board and a silver fork encrusted with the stuff lay beside them. There were saucers all over the floor with milk which had evaporated in the heat leaving yellow rings. Everything was untidy. He set his glass between a pile of magazines and a marmalade pot on the table. She asked him his name and about his school and where he lived and about his father.

Neil knew that his mother would call her nosey but he thought that she seemed interested in all his answers. She listened intently, blinking and staring at him with her face slightly turned as if she had a deaf ear.

'My father died a long time ago,' he said.

'And your mother?'

'She's alive.'

'And what does she do for a living?'

'She works in the cinema.'

'Oh how interesting. Is she an actress?'

'No. She just works there. With a torch. She gets me in free — for films that are suitable for me. Sometimes I take my friend Michael with me.'

'Is that the boy below?'

'Yes.'

'I thought his name was Benjamin. But how marvellous that you can see all these films free.' She clapped her ringed hands together and seemed genuinely excited. 'I used to love the cinema. The cartoons were my favourite. And the newsreels. I'll bet you're very popular when a good picture comes to town.'

'Yes I am,' said Neil and smiled and sipped his tonic.

'Let's go outside and talk. It's a shame to waste such a day in here.' Neil offered his arm as she lowered herself from the step to the ground.

'What a polite young man.'

'That's my mother's fault.'

They sat on the deckchairs facing the sun and she lit a cigarette, holding it between her jewelled fingers. Her face was brown and criss-crossed with wrinkles.

'Why aren't you swimming on such a day?' she asked.

Neil hesitated, then heard himself say, 'I can't. I've got a disease.'

'What is it?'

Again he paused but this old woman seemed to demand the truth.

'A thing — on my chest.'

'Let me see?' she said and leaned forward. He was amazed to find himself unbuttoning his shirt and showing her his mark. In the sunlight it didn't look so red. She scrutinized it and hummed, pursing her mouth and biting her lower lip.

'Why does it stop you bathing?'

Neil shrugged and began to button up when she stopped him

'Let the sun at it. I'm sure it can do no harm.' He left his shirt lying open. 'When I was in Africa I worked with lepers.'

'Lepers?'

'Yes, So the sight of you doesn't worry me,' she said. 'Watch that you don't suffer from more than just the disease.'

'I don't understand.'

'It's bad enough having it without being shy about it as well.'

'Have you got leprosy now?'

'No. It's not as contagious as everybody says.'

Neil finished his tonic and lay back in the chair. The sun was bright and hot on his chest. He listened to Mrs Wan talking about leprosy, of how the lepers lost their fingers and toes, not because of the disease but because they had lost all feeling in them and they broke and damaged them without knowing. Eventually they got gangrene. Almost all the horrible things of leprosy, she said, were secondary. Suddenly he heard Michael's voice.

'Mrs Wan, Mum says could you tell her where. . .' his voice tailed off seeing Neil's chest, '. . . the cheese grater is?'

'Do you know, I think I brought it up here.' She got up and stepped slowly into the caravan. Neil closed over his shirt and began to button it. Neither boy said a word.

At tea Michael spoke to him as if they were friends again and in bed that night it was Neil's suggestion that they go for a swim.

'Now? Are you mad?'

'They say it's warmer at night.'

'Yeah and we could make dummies in the beds like Clint Eastwood.'

'They don't *have* to look like Clint Eastwood.' They both laughed quiet sneezing laughs.

After one o'clock they dropped out of the window and ran to the beach. For almost half an hour in the pale darkness Neil thrashed and shivered. Eventually he sat down to wait in the warmer shallows, feeling the withdrawing sea hollow the sand around him. Further out, Michael whooped and rode the breakers like a shadow against their whiteness.

The Miraculous Candidate

At the age of fourteen John began to worry about the effects of his sanctity. The first thing had been a tingling, painful sensation in the palms of his hands and the soles of his feet. But an even more alarming symptom was the night when, as he fervently prayed himself to sleep, he felt himself being lifted up a full foot and a half above the bed — bedclothes and all. The next morning when he thought about it he dismissed it as a dream or the result of examination nerves.

Now on the morning of his Science exam he felt his stomach light and woolly, as if he had eaten feathers for breakfast. Outside the gym some of the boys fenced with new yellow rulers or sat drumming them on their knees. The elder ones, doing Senior and 'A' levels, stood in groups all looking very pale, one turning now and again to spit over his shoulder to show he didn't care. John checked for his examination card which his grandmother had carefully put in his inside pocket the night before. She had also pinned a Holy Ghost medal beneath his lapel where it wouldn't be seen and made him wear his blazer while she brushed it. She had asked him what Science was about and when John tried to explain she had interrupted him saying, 'If y'can blether as well with your pen — you'll do all right.'

One of the Seniors said it was nearly half-past and they all began to shuffle towards the door of the gym. John had been promised a watch if he passed his Junior.

The doors were opened and they all filed quietly to their places. John's desk was at the back with his number chalked

21 J 96, 839

on the top right-hand corner. He sat down, unclipped his fountain-pen and set it in the groove. All the desks had an empty hole for an ink-well. During the Maths exam one of the boys opposite who couldn't do any of the questions drew a face in biro on his finger and put it up through the hole and waggled it at John. He didn't seem to care whether he failed or not.

John sat looking at the wall-bars which lined the gym. The invigilator held up a brown paper parcel and pointed to the unbroken seal, then opened it, tearing off the paper noisily. He had a bad foot and some sort of high boot which squeaked every time he took a step. His face was pale and full of suspicion. He was always jumping up suddenly as if he had caught somebody on, flicking back his stringy hair as he did so. When he ate the tea and biscuits left at the door for him at eleven his eyes kept darting back and forward. John noticed that he 'gullied', a term his grandmother used for chewing and drinking tea at the same time. When reading, he never held the newspaper up but laid it flat on the table and stood propped on his arms, his big boot balanced on its toe to take the weight off it.

'If you ever meet the devil you'll know him by his cloven hoof,' his Granny had told him. A very holy woman, she had made it her business to read to him every Sunday night from the lives of the Saints, making him sit at her feet as she did so. While she read she let her glasses slip down to the end of her long nose and would look over them every so often, to see if he was listening. She had a mole on her chin with a hair like a watch-spring growing out of it. She read in a serious voice, very different to her ordinary one, and always blew on the fine tissuey pages to separate them before turning over with her trembling fingers. She had great faith and had a particular saint for every difficulty. 'St Blaise is good for throats and if you've ever lost anything St Anthony'll find it for you.' She always kept a sixpence under the statue of the Child of Prague because then, she said, she'd never be without. Above all there was St Joseph of Cupertino. For examinations he was your man. Often she read his bit out of the book to John.

'Don't sit with your back to the fire or you'll melt the marrow of your bones,' and he'd change his position at her feet and listen intently.

St Joseph was so close to God that sometimes when he prayed he was lifted up off the ground. Other times when he'd be carrying plates — he was only smart enough to work in the kitchen — he would go into a holy trance and break every dish on the tiled floor. He wanted to become a priest but he was very stupid so he learned off just one line of the Bible. But here — and this was the best part of the story — when his exam came didn't God make the Bishop ask him the one line he knew and he came through with flying colours. When the story was finished his Granny always said, 'It was all he was fit for, God help him — the one line.'

The invigilator squeaked his way down towards John and flicked a pink exam paper onto his desk. John steadied it with his hand. His eyes raced across the lines looking for the familiar questions. The feathers whirlpooled almost into his throat. He panicked. There was not a single question — *not one* — he knew anything about. He tried to settle himself and concentrated to read the first question.

State Newton's Universal Law of Gravitation. Give arguments for or against the statement that 'the only reason an apple falls downwards to meet the earth instead of the earth falling upwards to meet the apple is that the earth, being much more massive exerts the greater pull.' The mass of the moon is one eighty-first, and its radius one quarter that of the earth. What is the acceleration of gravity at its surface if. . .

It was no use. He couldn't figure out what was wrong. He had been to mass and communion every day for the past year — he had prayed hard for the right questions. The whole family had prayed hard for the right questions. What sort of return was this? He suppressed the thought because it was. . . it was God's will. Perhaps a watch would lead him into sin somehow or other?

He looked round at the rest of the boys. Most of them were writing frantically. Others sat sucking their pens or doodling on their rough-work sheets. John looked at the big clock they had hung on the wall-bars with its second hand slowly spinning. Twenty minutes had gone already and he hadn't put pen to paper. He must do *something*.

He closed his eyes very tight and clenching his fists to the side of his head he placed himself in God's hands and began to pray. His Granny's voice came to him. 'The Patron Saint of Examinations. Pray to him if you're really stuck'. He saw the shining damp of his palms, then pressed them to his face. Now he summoned up his whole being, focused it to a point of white heat. All the good that he had ever done, that he ever would do, all his prayers, the sum total of himself, he concentrated into the name of the Saint. He clenched his eyes so hard there was a roaring in his ears. His finger-nails bit into his cheeks. His lips moved and he said, 'Saint Joseph of Cupertino, help me.'

He opened his eyes and saw that somehow he was above his desk. Not far — he was raised up about a foot and a half, his body still in a sitting position. The invigilator looked up from his paper and John tried to lower himself back down into his seat. But he had no control over his limbs. The invigilator came round his desk quickly and walked towards him over the coconut matting, his boot creaking as he came.

'What are you up to?' he hissed between his teeth.

'Nothing,' whispered John. He could feel his cheeks becoming more and more red, until his whole face throbbed with blushing.

'Are you trying to copy?' The invigilator's face was on a level with the boy's. 'You can see every word the boy in front of you is writing, can't you?'

'No sir, I'm not trying to. . .' stammered John. 'I was just praying and. . .' The man looked like a Protestant. The Ministry brought in teachers from other schools. Protestant schools. He wouldn't understand about Saints.

'I don't care what you say you were doing. I think you are trying to copy and if you don't come down from there I'll have you disqualified.' The little man was getting as red in the face as John.

'I can't sir.'

24

'Very well then.' The invigilator clicked his tongue angrily and walked creak-padding away to his desk.

John again concentrated his whole being, focused it to a prayer of white heat.

'Saint Joseph of Cupertino. *Get me down please.*' But nothing happened. The invigilator lifted his clip-board with the candidates' names and started back towards John. Some of the boys in the back row had stopped writing and were laughing. The invigilator reached him.

'Are you going to come down from there or not?'

'I can't.' The tears welled up in John's eyes.

'Then I shall have to ask you to leave.'

'I can't,' said John.

The invigilator leaned forward and tapped the boy in front of John on the shoulder.

'Do you mind for a moment?' he said and turned the boy's answer paper face downwards on the desk. While he was turned away John frantically tried to think of a way out. His prayer hadn't worked. . . maybe a sin would. . . the invigilator turned to him.

'For the last time I'm. . .'

'Fuck the Pope,' said John and as he did so, he plumped back down into his seat skinning his shin on the tubular frame of the desk.

'Pardon. What did you say?' asked the invigilator.

'Nothing sir. It's all right now. I'm sorry sir.'

'What *is* wrong with you boy?'

'I can't do it, sir — any of it.' John pointed to the paper. The invigilator spun it round with his finger.

'You should have thought of that some months ago. . .' The words faded away. 'I'm very sorry. Just a minute,' he said, limping very quickly down to his desk. He came back with a white exam paper which he put in front of John.

'Very sorry,' he repeated. 'It does happen sometimes.'

John looked for the first time at the head of the pink paper. ADVANCED LEVEL PHYSICS. Now he read quickly through the questions on the white paper the invigilator had brought him. They were all there. Archimedes in his bath, properties of NaCl, allotropes of sulphur, the anatomy of the buttercup. The invigilator smiled with his spade-like teeth.

'Is that any better?' he asked. John nodded. '. . . and if you need some extra time to make up, you can have it.'

'Thank you sir,' said John. The invigilator hunkered down beside him and whispered confidentially.

'This wee mix-up'll not go any farther than between ourselves, will it. . .' He looked down at his clip-board. '. . . Johnny?'

'No sir.'

He gave John a pat on the back and creaked away over the coconut matting. John put his head down on the desk and uttered a prayer of Thanksgiving to St Joseph of Cupertino, this time making sure to keep his fervour within bounds.

A Time to Dance

Nelson, with a patch over one eye, stood looking idly into Mothercare's window. The sun was bright behind him and made a mirror out of the glass. He looked at his patch with distaste and felt it with his finger. The Elastoplast was rough and dry and he disliked the feel of it. Bracing himself for the pain, he ripped it off and let a yell out of him. A woman looked down at him curiously to see why he had made a noise, but by that time he had the patch in his pocket. He knew without looking that some of his eyebrow would be on it.

He had spent most of the morning in the Gardens avoiding distant uniforms, but now that it was coming up to lunchtime he braved it on the street. He had kept his patch on longer than usual because his mother had told him the night before that if he didn't wear it he would go 'stark, staring blind'.

Nelson was worried because he knew what it was like to be blind. The doctor at the eye clinic had given him a box of patches that would last for most of his lifetime. Opticludes. One day Nelson had worn two and tried to get to the end of the street and back. It was a terrible feeling. He had to hold his head back in case it bumped into anything and keep waving his hands in front of him backwards and forwards like windscreen wipers. He kept tramping on tin cans and heard them trundle emptily away. Broken glass crackled under his feet and he could not figure out how close to the wall he was. Several times he heard footsteps approaching, slowing down as if they were going to attack him in his

27

helplessness, then walking away. One of the footsteps even laughed. Then he heard a voice he knew only too well.

'Jesus, Nelson, what are you up to this time?' It was his mother. She led him back to the house with her voice blaring in his ear.

She was always shouting. Last night, for instance, she had started into him for watching T.V. from the side. She had dragged him round to the chair in front of it.

'That's the way the manufacturers make the sets. They put the picture on the front. But oh no, that's not good enough for our Nelson. He has to watch it from the side. Squint, my arse, you'll just go blind — stark, staring blind.'

Nelson had then turned his head and watched it from the front. She had never mentioned the blindness before. Up until now all she had said was, 'If you don't wear them patches that eye of yours will turn in till it's looking at your brains. God knows, not that it'll have much to look at.'

His mother was Irish. That was why she had a name like Skelly. That was why she talked funny. But she was proud of the way she talked and nothing angered her more than to hear Nelson saying 'Ah ken' and 'What like is it?' She kept telling him that someday they were going back, when she had enough ha'pence scraped together. 'Until then I'll not let them make a Scotchman out of you.' But Nelson talked the way he talked.

His mother had called him Nelson because she said she thought that his father had been a seafaring man. The day the boy was born she had read an article in the *Reader's Digest* about Nelson Rockefeller, one of the richest men in the world. It seemed only right to give the boy a good start. She thought it also had the advantage that it couldn't be shortened, but she was wrong. Most of the boys in the scheme called him Nelly Skelly.

He wondered if he should sneak back to school for dinner then skive off again in the afternoon. They had good dinners at school — like a hotel, with choices. Chips and magic things like rhubarb crumble. There was one big dinner-woman who gave him extra every time she saw him. She told him he needed fattening. The only drawback to the whole system was that he was on free dinners. Other people in his class were given their dinner money and it was up to them whether they went without a dinner and bought Coke and sweets and stuff with the money. It was a choice Nelson didn't have, so he had to invent other things to get the money out of his mother. In Lent there were the Black Babies; library fines were worth the odd 10p, although, as yet, he had not taken a book from the school library — and anyway they didn't have to pay fines, even if they were late; the Home Economics Department asked them to bring in money to buy their ingredients and Nelson would always add 20p to it.

'What the hell are they teaching you to cook — sides of beef?' his mother would yell. Outdoor pursuits required extra money. But even though they had ended after the second term, Nelson went on asking for the 50p on a Friday — 'to go horse riding'. His mother would never part with money without a speech of some sort.

'Horse riding? Horse riding! Jesus, I don't know what sort of school I've sent you to. Is Princess Anne in your class or something? Holy God, horse riding.'

Outdoor pursuits was mostly walking round museums on wet days and, when it was dry, the occasional trip to Portobello beach to write on a flapping piece of foolscap the signs of pollution you could see. Nelson felt that the best outdoor pursuit of the lot was what he was doing now. Skiving. At least that way you could do what you liked.

He groped in his pocket for the change out of his 50p and went into the shop. He bought a giant thing of bubble-gum and crammed it into his mouth. It was hard and dry at first and he couldn't answer the woman when she spoke to him.

'Whaaungh?'

'Pick the paper off the floor, son! Use the basket.'

He picked the paper up and screwed it into a ball. He aimed to miss the basket, just to spite her, but it went in. By the time he reached the bottom of the street the gum was chewy. He thrust his tongue into the middle of it and blew. A small disappointing bubble burst with a plip. It was not until the far end of Princes Street that he managed to blow big ones, pink and wobbling, that he could see at the end of his nose, which burst well and had to be gathered in shreds from his chin.

Then suddenly the crowds of shoppers parted and he saw his mother. In the same instant she saw him. She was on him before he could even think of running. She grabbed him by the fur of his parka and began screaming into his face.

'In the name of God, Nelson, what are you doing here? Why aren't you at school?' She began shaking him. 'Do you realise what this means? They'll put me in bloody jail. It'll be bloody Saughton for me, and no mistake,' She had her teeth gritted together and her mouth was slanting in her face. Then Nelson started to shout.

'Help! Help!' he yelled.

A woman with an enormous chest like a pigeon stopped. 'What's happening?' she said.

Nelson's mother turned on her. 'It's none of your bloody business.'

'I'm being kidnapped,' yelled Nelson.

'Young woman. Young woman. . .' said the lady with the large chest, trying to tap Nelson's mother on the shoulder with her umbrella, but Mrs Skelly turned with such a snarl that the woman edged away hesitatingly and looked over her shoulder and tut-tutted just loudly enough for the passing crowd to hear her.

'Help! I'm being kidnapped,' screamed Nelson, but everybody walked past looking the other way. His mother squatted down in front of him, still holding on to his jacket. She lowered her voice and tried to make it sound reasonable.

'Look Nelson, love. Listen. If you're skiving school, do you realise what'll happen to me? In Primary the Children's Panel threatened to send me to court. You're only at that Secondary and already that Sub-Attendance Committee thing wanted to fine me. Jesus, if you're caught again. . .'

Nelson stopped struggling. The change in her tone had quietened him down. She straightened up and looked wildly about her, wondering what to do.

'You've got to go straight back to school, do you hear me?'
'Yes.'

'Promise me you'll go.' The boy looked down at the ground. 'Promise?' The boy made no answer.

'I'll kill if you don't go back. I'd take you myself only I've my work to go to. I'm late as it is.'

Again she looked around as if she would see someone who would suddenly help her. Still she held on to his jacket. She was biting her lip.

'Oh God, Nelson.'

The boy blew a flesh-pink bubble and snapped it between his teeth. She shook him.

'That bloody bubble-gum.'

There was a loud explosion as the one o'clock gun went off. They both leapt.

'Oh Jesus, that gun puts the heart sideways in me every time it goes off. Come on, son, you'll have to come with me. I'm late. I don't know what they'll say when they see you but I'm bloody taking you to school by the ear. You hear me?'

She began rushing along the street, Nelson's sleeve in one hand, her carrier bag in the other. The boy had to run to keep from being dragged.

'Don't you dare try a trick like that again. Kidnapped, my arse. Nelson, if I knew somebody who would kidnap you — I'd pay *him* the money. Embarassing me on the street like that.'

They turned off the main road and went into a hallway and up carpeted stairs which had full-length mirrors along one side. Nelson stopped to make faces at himself but his mother chugged at his arm. At the head of the stairs stood a fat man in his shirtsleeves.

'What the hell is this?' he said. 'You're late, and what the hell is that?' He looked down from over his stomach at Nelson.

'I'll explain later,' she said. 'I'll make sure he stays in the room.'

'You should be on *now*,' said the fat man and turned and walked away through the swing doors. They followed him and Nelson saw, before his mother pushed him into the room, that it was a bar, plush and carpeted with crowds of men standing drinking.

'You sit here, Nelson, until I'm finished and then I'm taking you back to that school. You'll get nowhere if you don't do your lessons. I have to get changed now.'

She set her carrier bag on the floor and kicked off her shoes. Nelson sat down, watching her. She stopped and looked over her shoulder at him, biting her lip.

'Where's that bloody eyepatch you should be wearing?' Nelson indicated his pocket.

'Well, wear it then.' Nelson took the crumpled patch from his pocket, tugging bits of it unstuck to get it flat before he stuck it over his bad eye. His mother took out her handbag and began rooting about at the bottom of it. Nelson heard the rattle of her bottles of scent and tubes of lipstick.

'Ah,' she said and produced another eyepatch, flicking it clean. 'Put another one on till I get changed. I don't want you noseying at me.' She came to him, pulling away the white backing to the patch, and stuck it over his remaining eye. He imagined her concentrating, the tip of her tongue stuck out. She pressed his eyebrows with her thumbs, making sure that the patches were stuck.

'Now don't move, or you'll bump into something.'

Nelson heard the slither of her clothes and her small grunts as she hurriedly got changed. Then he heard her rustle in her bag, the soft pop and rattle as she opened her capsules. Her 'tantalisers' she called them, small black and red torpedoes. Then he heard her voice.

'Just you stay like that till I come back. That way you'll come to no harm. You hear me, Nelson? If I come back in here and you have those things off, I'll *kill* you. I'll not be long.'

Nelson nodded from his darkness.

'The door will be locked, so there's no running away.'

'Ah ken.'

Suddenly his darkness exploded with lights as he felt her bony hand strike his ear.

'You don't ken things, Nelson. You *know* them.'

He heard her go out and the key turn in the lock. His ear sang and he felt it was hot. He turned his face up to the ceiling. She had left the light on because he could see pinkish through the patches. He smelt the beer and stale smoke. Outside the room pop music had started up, very loudly. He heard the deep notes pound through to where he sat. He felt his ear with his hand and it *was* hot.

Making small *aww* sounds of excruciating pain, he slowly detached both eyepatches from the bridge of the nose outwards. In case his mother should come back he did not take them off completely, but left them hinged to the sides of his eyes. When he turned to look around they flapped like blinkers.

It wasn't really a room, more a broom cupboard. Crates were stacked against one wall; brushes and mops and buckets stood near a very low sink; on a row of coat-hooks hung some limp raincoats and stained white jackets; his mother's stuff hung on the last hook. The floor was covered with tramped-flat cork tips. Nelson got up to look at what he was sitting on. It was a crate of empties. He went to the keyhole and looked out, but all he could see was a patch of wallpaper opposite. Above the door was a narrow window. He looked up at it, his eyepatches falling back to touch his ears. He went over to the sink and had a drink of water from the low tap, sucking noisily at the column of water as it splashed into the sink. He stopped and wiped his mouth. The water felt cold after the mint of the bubble-gum. He looked up at his mother's things, hanging on the hook; her tights and drawers were as she wore them, but inside out and hanging knock-kneed on top of everything. In her bag he found her blonde wig and tried it on, smelling the perfume of it as he did so. At home he liked noseying in his mother's room; smelling all her bottles of make-up; seeing her spangled things. He had to stand on the crate to see himself but the mirror was all brown measles under its surface and the eyepatches ruined the effect. He sat down again and began pulling at the bubble-gum, seeing how long he could make it stretch before it broke. Still the music pounded outside. It was so loud the vibrations tickled his feet. He sighed and looked up at the window again.

If his mother took him back to school, he could see problems. For starting St John the Baptist's she had bought him a brand new Adidas bag for his books. Over five pounds it had cost her, she said. On his first real skive he had dumped the bag in the bin at the bottom of his stair, every morning for a week, and travelled light into town. On the Friday he came home just in time to see the bin lorry driving away in a cloud of bluish smoke. He had told his mother that the bag had been stolen from the playground during break. She had threatened to phone the school about it but Nelson had hastily assured her that the whole matter was being investigated by none other than the Headmaster himself. This threat put the notion out of his head of asking her for the money to replace the books. At that point he had not decided on a figure. He could maybe try it again some time when all the fuss had died down. But now it was all going to be stirred if his mother took him to school.

He pulled two crates to the door and climbed up but they were not high enough. He put a third now on top, climbed on again, and gingerly straightened, balancing on its rim. On tip-toe he could see out. He couldn't see his mother anywhere. He saw a crowd of men standing in a semicircle. Behind them were some very bright lights, red, yellow and blue. They all had pints in their hands which they didn't seem to be drinking. They were all watching something which Nelson couldn't see. Suddenly the music stopped and the men all began drinking and talking. Standing on tip-toe for so long, Nelson's legs began to shake and he heard the bottles in the crate rattle. He rested for a moment. Then the music started again. He looked to see. The men now just stood looking. It was as if they were seeing a ghost. Then they all cheered louder than the music.

Nelson climbed down and put the crates away from the door so that his mother could get in. He closed his eyepatches over for a while, but still she didn't come. He listened to another record, this time a slow one. He decided to travel blind to get another drink of water. As he did so the music changed to fast. He heard the men cheering again, then the rattle of the key in the lock. Nelson, his arms rotating in front of him, tried to make his way back to the crate. His mother's voice said, 'Don't you dare take those eyepatches off.' Her voice was panting. Then his hand hit up against her. It was her bare stomach, hot and damp with sweat. She guided him to sit down, breathing heavily through her nose.

'I'll just get changed and then you're for school right away, boy.' Nelson nodded. He heard her light a cigarette as she dressed. When she had finished she ripped off his right eyepatch.

'There now, we're ready to go,' she said, ignoring Nelson's anguished yells.

'That's the wrong eye,' he said.

'Oh shit,' said his mother and ripped off the other one, turned it upside down and stuck it over his right eye. The smoke from the cigarette in her mouth trickled up into her eye and she held it half shut. Nelson could see the bright points of sweat shining through her make-up. She still hadn't got her breath back fully yet. She smelt of drink.

On the way out, the fat man with the rolled-up sleeves held out two fivers and Nelson's mother put them into her purse.

'The boy — never again,' he said, looking down at Nelson.

They took the Number Twelve to St John the Baptist's. It was the worst possible time because, just as they were going in, the bell rang for the end of a period and suddenly the quad was full of pupils, all looking at Nelson and his mother. Some sixth-year boys wolf-whistled after her and others stopped to stare. Nelson felt a flush of pride that she was causing a stir. She was dressed in black satiny jeans, very tight, and her pink blouse was knotted, leaving her tanned midriff bare. They went into the office and a secretary came up to the window.

'Yes?' she said, looking Mrs Skelly up and down.

'I'd like to see the Head,' she said.

'I'm afraid he's at a meeting. What is it about?'

'About him.' She waved her thumb over her shoulder at Nelson.

'What year is he?'

'What year are you, son?' His mother turned to him.

'First.'

'First Year. Oh, then you'd best see Mr MacDermot, the First Year Housemaster.' The secretary directed them to Mr MacDermot's office. It was at the other side of the school and they had to walk what seemed miles of corridors before they found it. Mrs Skelly's stiletto heels clicked along the tiles.

'It's a wonder you don't get lost in here, son,' she said as she knocked on the Housemaster's door. Mr MacDermot opened it and invited them in. Nelson could see that he too was looking at her, his eyes wide and his face smiley.

'What can I do for you?' he said when they were seated.

'It's him,' said Mrs Skelly. 'He's been skiving again. I caught him this morning.'

'I see,' said Mr MacDermot. He was very young to be a Housemaster. He had a black moustache which he began to stroke with the back of his hand. He paused for a long time. Then he said, 'Remind me of your name, son.'

'— Oh, I'm sorry,' said Mrs Skelly. 'My name is Skelly and this is my boy Nelson.'

'Ah, yes, Skelly.' The Housemaster got up and produced a yellow file from the filing cabinet. 'You must forgive me, but we haven't seen a great deal of Nelson lately.'

'Do you mind if I smoke?' asked Mrs Skelly.

'Not at all, said the Housemaster, getting up to open the window.

'The trouble is, that the last time we were at the Sub-Attendance Committee thing they said they would take court action if it happened again. And it has.'

'Well, it may not come to that with the Attendance Sub-Committee. If we nip it in the bud. If Nelson makes an effort, isn't that right, Nelson?' Nelson sat silent.

'Speak when the master's speaking to you,' yelled Mrs Skelly.

'Yes,' said Nelson, making it barely audible.

'You're Irish too,' said Mrs Skelly to the Housemaster, smiling.

'That's right,' said Mr MacDermot. 'I thought your accent was familiar. Where do you come from?'

'My family come from just outside Derry. And you?'

'Oh, that's funny. I'm just across the border from you. Donegal.' As they talked, Nelson stared out the window. He had never heard his mother so polite. He could just see a corner of the playing fields and a class coming out with the Gym teacher. Nelson hated Gym more than anything. It was crap. He loathed the changing rooms, the getting stripped in front of others, the stupidity he felt when he missed the ball. The smoke from his mother's cigarette went in an arc towards the open window. Distantly he could hear the class shouting as they started a game of football.

'Nelson! Isn't that right?' said Mr MacDermot loudly.

'What?'

'That even when you are here you don't work hard enough.'

'Hmmm,' said Nelson.

'You don't have to tell me,' said his mother. 'It's not just his eye that's lazy. If you ask me the whole bloody lot of him is. I've never seen him washing a dish in his life and he leaves everything at his backside.

'Yes,' said the Housemaster. Again he stroked his moustache. 'What is required from Nelson is a change of attitude. Attitude, Nelson. You understand a word like attitude?'

'Yes.'

'He's just not interested in school, Mrs Skelly.'

'I've no room to talk, of course. I had to leave at fifteen,' she said, rolling her eyes in Nelson's direction. 'You know what I mean? Otherwise I might have stayed on and got my exams.'

'I see,' said Mr MacDermot. 'Can we look forward to a change in attitude, Nelson?'

'Hm-m.'

'Have you no friends in school?' asked the Housemaster.

'Naw.'

'And no interest. You see, you can't be interested in any subject unless you do some work at it. Work pays dividends with interest. . .' he paused and looked at Mrs Skelly. She was inhaling her cigarette. He went on, 'Have you considered the possibility that Nelson may be suffering from school phobia?'

Mrs Skelly looked at him. 'Phobia, my arse,' she said. 'He just doesn't like school.'

'I see. Does he do any work at home then?'

'Not since he had his bag with all his books in it stolen.'

'Stolen?'

Nelson leaned forward in his chair and said loudly and clearly, 'I'm going to try to be better from now on. I am. I am going to try, sir.'

'That's more like it,' said the Housemaster, also edging forward.

'I am not going to skive. I am going to try. Sir, I'm going to do my best.'

'Good boy. I think, Mrs Skelly, if I have a word with the right people and convey to them what we have spoken about, I think there will be no court action. Leave it with me, will you? And I'll see what I can do. Of course it all depends on Nelson. If he is as good as his word. One more truancy and I'll be forced to report it. And he must realise that he has three full years of school to do before he leaves us. You must be aware of my position in this matter. You understand what I'm saying, Nelson?'

'Ah ken,' he said. 'I know.'

'You go off to you class now. I have some more things to say to your mother.'

Nelson rose to his feet and shuffled towards the door. He stopped.

'Where do I go, sir?'

'Have you not got your timetable?'

'No sir. Lost it.'

The Housemaster, tut-tutting, dipped into another file, read a card and told him that he should be at R.K. in Room 72. As he left, Nelson noticed that his mother had put her knee up against the chair, as she took out another cigarette.

'Bye, love,' she said.

When he went into Room 72 there was a noise of oos and ahhs from the others in the class. He said to the teacher that he had been seeing Mr MacDermot. She gave him a Bible and told him to sit down. He didn't know her name. He had her for English as well as R.K. She was always rabbiting on about poetry.

'You, boy, that just came in. For your benefit, we are talking and reading about organisation. Page 667. About how we should divide our lives up with work and prayer. How we should put each part of the day to use, and each part of the year. This is one of the most beautiful passages in the whole of the Bible. Listen to its rhythms as I read.' She lightly drummed her closed fist on the desk in front of her.

38

' "There is an appointed time for everything, and a time for every affair under the heavens. A time to be born and a time to die; a time to plant and a time to uproot. . ." '

'What page did you say, Miss?' asked Nelson.

'Six-six-seven,' she snapped and read on, her voice trembling, ' "A time to kill and a time to heal; a time to wear down and time to build. A time to weep and a time to laugh; a time to mourn and a time to dance. . ." '

Nelson looked out of the window, at the tiny white H of the goal posts in the distance. He took his bubble-gum out and stuck it under the desk. The muscles of his jaw ached from chewing the now flavourless mass. He looked down at page 667 with its microscopic print, then put his face close to it. He tore off his eyepatch, thinking that if he was going to become blind then the sooner it happened the better.

A Rat and Some Renovations

Almost every one in Ireland must have experienced American visitors or, as we called them, 'The Yanks'. Just before we were visited for the first time, my mother decided to have the working kitchen modernised. We lived in a terrace of dilapidated Victorian houses whose front gardens measured two feet by the breadth of the house. The scullery, separated from the kitchen by a wall, was the same size as the garden, and just as arable. When we pulled out the vegetable cupboard we found three or four potatoes which had fallen down behind and taken root. Ma said, 'God, if the Yanks had seen that.'

She engaged the workmen early so the job would be finished and the newness worn off by the time the Yanks arrived. She said she wouldn't like them to think that she got it done up just for them.

The first day the workmen arrived they demolished the wall, ripped up the floor and left the cold water tap hanging four feet above the bucket. We didn't see them again for three weeks. Grandma kept trying to make excuses for them, saying that it was very strenuous work. My mother however managed to get them back and they worked for three days, erecting a sink unit and leaving a hole for the outlet pipe. It must have been through this hole that the rat got in.

The first signs were discovered by Ma in the drawer of the new unit. She called me and said, 'What's those?' I looked and saw six hard brown ovals trundling about the drawer.

'Ratshit,' I said. Ma backed disbelievingly away, her hands over her mouth, repeating, 'It's a mouse, it's mouse, it must be mouse.'

The man from next door, Mr Frank Twoomey, who had lived most of his life in the country, was called — he said from the size of them, it could well be a horse. At this my mother took her nightdress and toothbrush and moved in with an aunt across the street, leaving the brother and myself with the problem. Armed with a hatchet and shovel we banged and rattled the cupboards, then when we felt sure it was gone we blocked the hole with hardboard and sent word to Ma to return, that all was well.

It was after two days safety that she discovered the small brown bombs again. I met her with her nightdress under her arm, in the path. She just said, 'I found more,' and headed for her sister's.

That evening it was Grandma's suggestion that we should borrow the Grimleys' cat. The brother was sent and had to pull it from beneath the side-board because it was very shy of strangers. He carried it across the road and the rat-killer was so terrified of the traffic and Peter squeezing it that it peed all down his front. By this time Ma's curiosity had got the better of her and she ventured from her sister's to stand pale and nervous in our path. The brother set the cat down and turned to look for a cloth to wipe himself. The cat shot past him down the hall,. past Ma who screamed, 'Jesus, the rat', and leapt into the hedge. The cat ran until a bus stopped it with a thud. The Grimleys haven't spoken to us since.

Ma had begun to despair. 'What age do rats live to?' she asked. 'And what'll we do if it's still here when the Yanks come?' Peter said that they loved pigs in the kitchen.

The next day we bought stuff, pungent like phosphorous and spread it on cubes of bread. The idea of this stuff was to roast the rat inside when he ate it so that he would drink himself to death.

'Just like Uncle Matt,' said Peter. He tactlessly read out the instructions to Grandma who then came out in sympathy with the rat. Ma thought it may have gone outside, so to make sure, we littered the yard with pieces

41

of bread as well. In case it didn't work Ma decided to do a novena of masses so she got up the next morning and on the driveway to the chapel which runs along the back of our house she noticed six birds with their feet in the air, stone dead.

Later that day the rat was found in the same condition on the kitchen floor. It was quickly buried in the dust-bin using the shovel as a hearse. The next day the workmen came, finished the job, and the Yanks arrived just as the paint was drying.

They looked strangely out of place with their brown, leathery faces, rimless glasses and hat brims flamboyantly large, as we met them at the boat. . . Too summery by half, against the dripping eaves of the sheds at the dock-yard. At home by a roaring fire on a July day, after having laughed a little at the quaintness of the taxi, they exchanged greetings, talked about family likenesses, jobs, and then dried up. For the next half hour the conversation had to be manufactured, except for a comparison of education systems which was confusing and therefore lasted longer. Then everything stopped.

The brother said, 'I wouldn't call this an embarassing silence.'

They all laughed, nervously dispelling the silence but not the embarrassment.

Ma tried to cover up. 'Would yous like another cup of cawfee?' Already she had begun to pick up the accent. They agreed and the oldish one with the blue hair followed her out to the kitchen.

'Gee, isn't this madern,' she said.

Ma, untacking her hand from the paint on the drawer, said, 'Yeah, we done it up last year.'

Secrets

He had been called to be there at the end. His Great Aunt Mary had been dying for some days now and the house was full of relatives. He had just left his girlfriend's home — they had been studying for 'A' levels together — and had come back to the house to find all the lights spilling onto the lawn and a sense of purpose which had been absent from the last few days.

He knelt at the bedroom door to join in the prayers. His knees were on the wooden threshold and he edged them forward onto the carpet. They had tried to wrap her fingers around a crucifix but they kept loosening. She lay low on the pillow and her face seemed to have shrunk by half since he had gone out earlier in the night. Her white hair was damped and pushed back from her forehead. She twisted her head from side to side, her eyes closed. The prayers chorused on, trying to cover the sound she was making deep in her throat. Someone said about her teeth and his mother leaned over her and said, 'That's the pet', and took her dentures from her mouth. The lower half of her face seemed to collapse. She half opened her eyes but could not raise her eyelids enough and showed only crescents of white.

'Hail Mary full of grace. . .' the prayers went on. He closed his hands over his face so that he would not have to look but smelt the trace of his girlfriend's handcream from his hands. The noise, deep and guttural, that his aunt was making became intolerable to him. It was as if she were drowning. She had lost all the dignity he knew her to have. He got up from the floor and stepped between the others

43

who were kneeling and went into her sitting-room off the same landing.

He was trembling with anger or sorrow, he didn't know which. He sat in the brightness of her big sitting-room at the oval table and waited for something to happen. On the table was a cut-glass vase of irises, dying because she had been in bed for over a week. He sat staring at them. They were withering from the tips inward, scrolling themselves delicately, brown and neat. Clearing up after themselves. He stared at them for a long time until he heard the sounds of women weeping from the next room.

His aunt had been small — her head on a level with his when she sat at her table — and she seemed to get smaller each year. Her skin fresh, her hair white and waved and always well washed. She wore no jewelry except a cameo ring on the third finger of her right hand and, around her neck, a gold locket on a chain. The white classical profile on the ring was almost worn through and had become translucent and indistinct. The boy had noticed the ring when she had read to him as a child. In the beginning fairy tales, then as he got older extracts from famous novels, *Lorna Doone, Persuasion, Wuthering Heights* and her favourite extract, because she read it so often, Pip's meeting with Miss Havisham from *Great Expectations*. She would sit with him on her knee, her arms around him and holding the page flat with her hand. When he was bored he would interrupt her and ask about the ring. He loved hearing her tell of how her grandmother had given it to her as a brooch and she had had a ring made from it. He would try to count back to see how old it was. Had her grandmother got it from *her* grandmother? And if so what had she turned it into? She would nod her head from side to side and say, 'How would I know a thing like that?' keeping her place in the closed book with her finger.

'Don't be so inquisitive,' she'd say. 'Let's see what happens next in the story.'

One day she was sitting copying figures into a long narrow book with a dip pen when he came into her room. She didn't look up but when he asked her a question she

44

just said, 'Mm?' and went on writing. The vase of irises on the oval table vibrated slightly as she wrote.

'What is it?' She wiped the nib on blotting paper and looked up at him over her reading glasses.

'I've started collecting stamps and Mamma says you might have some.'

'Does she now —?'

She got up from the table and went to the tall walnut bureau-bookcase standing in the alcove. From a shelf of the bookcase she took a small wallet of keys and selected one for the lock. There was a harsh metal shearing sound as she pulled the desk flap down. The writing area was covered with green leather which had dog-eared at the corners. The inner part was divided into pigeon holes, all bulging with papers. Some of them, envelopes, were gathered in batches nipped at the waist with elastic bands. There were postcards and bills and cash-books. She pointed to the postcards.

'You may have the stamps on those,' she said. 'But don't tear them. Steam them off.'

She went back to the oval table and continued writing. He sat on the arm of the chair looking through the picture post-cards — torchlight processions at Lourdes, brown photographs of town centres, dull black and whites of beaches backed by faded hotels. Then he turned them over and began to sort the stamps. Spanish, with a bald man, French with a rooster, German with funny jerky print, some Italian with what looked like a chimney-sweep's bundle and a hatchet.

'These are great,' he said. 'I haven't got any of them.'

'Just be careful how you take them off.'

'Can I take them downstairs?'

'Is your mother there?'

'Yes.'

'Then perhaps it's best if you bring the kettle up here.'

He went down to the kitchen. His mother was in the morning room polishing silver. He took the kettle and the flex upstairs. Except for the dipping and scratching of his Aunt's pen the room was silent. It was at the back of the house overlooking the orchard and the sound of traffic from the main road was distant and muted. A tiny rattle began as the kettle warmed up, then it bubbled and steam gushed quietly from its spout. The cards began to curl slightly in the jet of steam but she didn't seem to be watching. The stamps peeled moistly off and he put them in a saucer of water to flatten them.

'Who is Brother Benignus?' he asked. She seemed not to hear. He asked again and she looked over her glasses.

'He was a friend.'

His flourishing signature appeared again and again. Sometimes Bro Benignus, sometimes Benignus and once Iggy.

'Is he alive?'

'No, he's dead now. Watch the kettle doesn't run dry.'

When he had all the stamps off he put the postcards together and replaced them in the pigeon-hole. He reached over towards the letters but before his hand touched them his aunt's voice, harsh for once, warned.

'A-A-A,' she moved her pen from side to side. 'Do-not-touch,' she said and smiled. 'Anything else, yes! That section, no!' She resumed her writing.

The boy went through some other papers and found some photographs. One was of a beautiful girl. It was very old-fashioned but he could see that she was beautiful. The picture was a pale brown oval set on a white square of card. The edges of the oval were misty. The girl in the photograph was young and had dark, dark hair scraped severely back and tied like a knotted rope on the top of her head — high arched eyebrows, her nose straight and thin, her mouth slightly smiling, yet not smiling — the way a mouth is after smiling. Her eyes looked out at him dark and knowing and beautiful.

'Who is that?' he asked.

'Why? What do you think of her?'

'She's all right.'

'Do you think she is beautiful?' The boy nodded.

'That's me,' she said. The boy was glad he had pleased her in return for the stamps.

Other photographs were there, not posed ones like Aunt Mary's but Brownie snaps of laughing groups of girls in bucket hats like German helmets and coats to their ankles. They seemed tiny faces covered in clothes. There was a photograph of a young man smoking a cigarette, his hair combed one way by the wind against a background of sea.

'Who is that in the uniform?' the boy asked.

'He's a soldier,' she answered without looking up.

'Oh,' said the boy. 'But who is he?'

'He was a friend of mine before you were born,' she said. Then added, 'Do I smell something cooking? Take your stamps and off you go. That's the boy.'

The boy looked at the back of the picture of the man and saw in black spidery ink 'John, Aug ' 15 Ballintoye'.

'I thought maybe it was Brother Benignus,' he said. She looked at him not answering.

'Was your friend killed in the war?'

At first she said no, but then she changed her mind.

'Perhaps he was,' she said, then smiled. 'You are far too inquisitive. Put it to use and go and see what is for tea. Your mother will need the kettle.' She came over to the bureau and helped tidy the photographs away. Then she locked it and put the keys on the shelf.

'Will you bring me up my tray?'

The boy nodded and left.

It was a Sunday evening, bright and summery. He was doing his homework and his mother was sitting on the carpet in one of her periodic fits of tidying out the drawers of the mahogany sideboard. On one side of her was a heap of paper scraps torn in quarters and bits of rubbish, on the other the useful items that had to be kept. The boy heard the bottom stair creak under Aunt Mary's light footstep. She knocked and put her head round the door and said that she was walking to Devotions. She was dressed in her good coat and hat and was just easing her fingers into her second glove. The boy saw her stop and pat her hair into place before the mirror in the hallway. His mother stretched over and slammed the door shut. It vibrated, then he heard the deeper sound of the outside door closing and her first few steps on the gravelled driveway. He sat for a long time wondering if he would have time or not. Devotions could take anything from twenty minutes to three quarters of an hour, depending on who was saying it.

Ten minutes must have passed, then the boy left his homework and went upstairs and into his aunt's sitting room. He stood in front of the bureau wondering, then he reached for the keys. He tried several before he got the right one. The desk flap screeched as he pulled it down. He pretended to look at the postcards again in case there were any stamps he had missed. Then he put them away and reached for the bundle of letters. The elastic band was thick and old, brittle almost and when he took it off its track remained on the wad of letters. He carefully opened one and took out the letter and unfolded it, frail, khaki-coloured.

My dearest Mary, it began, I am so tired I can hardly write to you. I have spent what seems like all day censoring letters (there is a howitzer about 100 yds away firing every 2 minutes). The letters are heartrending in their attempt to express what they cannot. Some of the men are illiterate, others almost so. I know that they feel as much as we do, yet they do not have the words to express it. That is your job in the schoolroom to give us generations who can read and write well. They have. . .

The boy's eye skipped down the page and over the next. He read the last paragraph.

Mary I love you as much as ever — more so that we cannot be together. I do not know which is worse, the hurt of this war or being separated from you. Give all my love to Brendan and all at home.

It was signed, scribbles with what he took to be John. He folded the paper carefully into its original creases and put it in the envelope. He opened another.

My love, it is thinking of you that keeps me sane. When I get a moment I open my memories of you as if I were reading. Your long dark hair — I always imagine you wearing the blouse with the tiny roses, the white one that opened down the back — your eyes that said so much without words, the way you lowered your head when I said anything that embarrassed you, and the clean nape of your neck.

The day I think about most was the day we climbed the head at Ballycastle. In a hollow, out of the wind, the air full of pollen and the sound of insects, the grass warm and dry and you lying beside me your hair undone, between me and the sun. You remember that that was where I first kissed you and the look of disbelief in your eyes that made me laugh afterwards.

It makes me laugh now to see myself savouring these memories standing alone up to my thighs in muck. It is everywhere, two, three feet deep. To walk ten yards leaves you quite breathless.

I haven't time to write more today so I leave you with my feet in the clay and my head in the clouds.
I love you, John.

He did not bother to put the letter back into the envelope but opened another.

My dearest, I am so cold that I find it difficult to keep my hand steady enough to write. You remember when we swam the last two fingers of your hand went the colour and texture of candles with the cold. Well that is how I am all over. It is almost four days since I had any real sensation in my feet or legs. Everything is frozen. The ground is like steel.

Forgive me telling you this but I feel I have to say it to someone. The worst thing is the dead. They sit or lie frozen in the position they die. You can distinguish them from the living because their faces are the colour of slate. God help us when the thaw comes. . . This war is beginning to have an effect on me. I have lost all sense of feeling. The only emotion I have experienced lately is one of anger. Sheer white trembling anger. I have no pity or sorrow for the dead and injured. I thank God it is not me but I am enraged that it had to be them. If I live through this experience I will be a different person.

The only thing that remains constant is my love for you.

Today a man died beside me. A piece of shrapnel had pierced his neck as we were moving under fire. I pulled him into a crater and stayed with him until he died. I watched him choke and then drown in his blood.

I am full of anger which has no direction.

He sorted through the pile and read half of some, all of others. The sun had fallen low in the sky and shone directly into the room onto the pages he was reading making the paper glare. He selected a letter from the back of the pile and shaded it with his hand as he read.

Dearest Mary, I am writing this to you from my hospital bed. I hope that you were not too worried about not hearing from me. I have been here, so they tell me, for two weeks and it took another two weeks before I could bring myself to write this letter.

I have been thinking a lot as I lie here about the war and about myself and about you. I do not know how to say this but I feel deeply that I must do something, must sacrifice something to make up for the horror of the past year. In some strange way Christ has spoken to me through the carnage. . .

Suddenly the boy heard the creak of the stair and he frantically tried to slip the letter back into its envelope but it crumpled and would not fit. He bundled them all together. He could hear his aunt's familiar puffing on the short stairs to her room. He spread the elastic band wide with his fingers. It snapped and the letters scattered. He pushed them into their pigeon hole and quickly closed the desk flap. The brass screeched loudly and clicked shut. At that moment his aunt came into the room.

'What are you doing boy?' she snapped.

'Nothing.' He stood with the keys in his hand. She walked to the bureau and opened it. The letters sprung out in an untidy heap.

'You have been reading my letters,' she said quietly. Her mouth was tight with the words and her eyes blazed. The boy could say nothing. She struck him across the side of the face.

'Get out,' she said. 'Get out of my room'

The boy, the side of his face stinging and red, put the keys on the table on his way out. When he reached the door she called him. He stopped, his hand on the handle.

'You are dirt,' she hissed, 'and always will be dirt. I shall remember this till the day I die.'

Even though it was a warm evening there was a fire in the large fireplace. His mother had asked him to light it so that she could clear out Aunt Mary's stuff. The room could then be his study, she said. She came in and seeing him at the table said, 'I hope I'm not disturbing you.'

'No.'

She took the keys from her pocket, opened the bureau and began burning papers and cards. She glanced quickly at each one before she flicked it onto the fire.

'Who was Brother Benignus?' he asked.

His mother stopped sorting and said, 'I don't know. Your aunt kept herself very much to herself. She got books from him through the post occasionally. That much I do know.'

She went on burning the cards. They built into strata, glowing red and black. Now and again she broke up the pile with the poker, sending showers of sparks up the chimney. He saw her come to the letters. She took off the elastic band and put it to one side with the useful things and began dealing the envelopes into the fire. She opened one and read quickly through it, then threw it on top of the burning pile.

'Mama,' he said.

'Yes?'

'Did Aunt Mary say anything about me?'

'What do you mean?'

'Before she died — did she say anything?'

'Not that I know of — the poor thing was too far gone to speak, God rest her.' She went on burning, lifting the corners of the letters with the poker to let the flames underneath them.

When he felt a hardness in his throat he put his head down on his books. Tears came into his eyes for the first time since she had died and he cried silently into the crook of his arm for the woman who had been his maiden aunt, his teller of tales, that she might forgive him.

Where the Tides Meet

We arrive at Torr Head about an hour before dusk and get out of the car. Three men, Christopher the boy, and the dog. Michael and Martin stand, their guns broken, loading them with bright, brick-red cartridges from their pockets. We have lost the dog's lead and I use a makeshift choker. It is an ordinary lead but I form a noose with the loop of the handle so that when he pulls too hard the noose tightens.

'For God's sake don't let him go,' they tell me. He is too eager and pulls me at a run when I want to walk. They tell me to tap him on the nose and shout 'heel' and he will respond. He is too eager. They keep their guns broken and climb the fence. The boy Christopher is excited and anxious and edges ahead to try and see. He is on tip-toe trying to see over the next rise. Michael, his father hisses at him, 'Keep behind the line of guns.' I walk behind all three with the dog. It is a black labrador called Ikabod. His tongue hangs out as he strains forward. I must be leaning at an angle of forty-five degrees trying to hold him. The makeshift lead is so embedded into the black folds of his neck that the only part of it visible is the taut line to my hand. The chain at my end bites deeply.

Suddenly Martin shouts, not a loud shout, not a loud shout, but a quiet urgent one, 'Mickey, to your right.'

Michael brings the gun up to his cheek, leans slightly forward, all balance. The sound is half way between a crack and a thud. The barrel jerks slightly as he fires. Both barrels. It is only then that I see the white scuts of two rabbits disappearing into some bushes on our right. At the sound of the gun Ikabod goes mad. He pulls me running and sliding down the hill. On the point of falling I decide to let him go. If Michael has hit one of the rabbits it must be the dog's job to retrieve. Ikabod disappears into the bushes, the lead whipping after him loosely. It is only then that I hear Michael shouting, 'Hold on to him.' I hear two more shots and my head ducks down into my coat, thinking Martin is shooting over my head at the same two rabbits, but when I look round he is shooting up the hill. I don't see what he is shooting at. I go down and look over the bush. It is a sloping cliff of rocks covered in bushes and grasses. Ikabod runs hither and thither looking for the rabbits. I whistle at him and he comes back. He is a good dog. Christopher is beside me looking over, 'Did he get one? Did he get one?' We catch up with the others.

I say defending myself, 'If you don't let him off after you shoot when *do* you let him off?'

'You don't,' says Michael.

'What did we bring him for then?' He doesn't answer. 'I thought he was supposed to be a retriever.'

'For birds,' says Michael and everybody laughs. Both men are pushing cartridges into their guns. We stand a while and talk, scanning the hillside yet knowing we have scared everything within earshot.

'You don't expect to see something that soon,' says Martin. Michael, who has been here many times before, points out the sea where the tides meet. Just beyond Torr Head the sea is white and swirling. Waves leap and crash together as if onto rocks but there are no rocks. This is about two hundred yards off-shore. They tell me it is the Irish sea coming up and the Gulf Stream coming down. In a boat they say you would have no chance.

We double back to a field on the actual Torr itself where they have seen rabbits before. Each fence they break their guns. Each fence Ikabod tries to go through the wire and me over it so that there is an elaborate disentangling and tugging each time. We have reached the field now and they walk in front of me, spread out, Christopher nearer to his father than Martin. The grass is coarse and long but flattened by the wind which must be constant in this place. It has the appearance of grass by a river in flood. The men walk with their guns at the ready, chest high. They stride, but stride quietly, their heads turning from side to side sweeping the landscape. I think to myself that they are like hunters and only then realise that that is what they are. We reach the Torr itself without seeing anything or a shot being fired. We stop and talk. Michael asks me if I would like a shot. I say yes, I let the dog off the lead, he runs mad.

'What is there to shoot at?' He points out an old fence post, a railway sleeper, at the edge of the cliff. He shows me the safety catch. I click it off and take aim. It has begun to get dark and the sea behind the post is slate grey. Flints of white from where the tides meet distract me. The butt seems remarkably close to my cheek and I know to expect the recoil of the gun. I am afraid of it and when I shoot I miss completely. We inspect the post. The noise of the explosion pinging still in my ears.

'I did hit it,' I say.

Michael looks closer. 'It's fucking woodworm.' He keeps his voice low so that the boy will not hear. The few small holes do look like woodworm. I go back and shoot the other barrel. I miss again. Martin has gone off looking for more rabbits. We hear a shot from over the brow of the hill. It sounds distorted, plucked away by the wind. Michael loads the gun and fires at the post. It gouges a small crater in the dead wood. Around the periphery when I look closely there are some holes like woodworm.

'Mine's a pint.'

It must be two fields before we notice that Ikabod isn't with us. We stand whistling and shouting but he does not come. We go back to the fence post and look all round, calling.

'Would he have gone over the cliff?' We climb the small fence edging very carefully down the slippy grass.

'Ik-a-bod, Ik-a-bod.' Then we hear a definite dog noise from below.

'He's there somewhere.' We do not know whether it is a cliff like the last one with bushes and outcrops and paths so we inch forward with care. I get to the edge first. It is a sheer drop. Emptiness for about two hundred feet. A rook sails past on a level with us. There is a rubble of rocks below on the beach. I see Ikabod lying on his side at the bottom. From then on we do not talk. To our right there is an accessible way down to the beach and we run. By now the boy and Martin have caught up with us. We half slide, half run down the slope holding onto the tussocky grass. When we get to the dog it is dead. I put my hand on its side and find it still warm. There is no heartbeat. Christopher talks incessantly asking, 'Is it dead, Daddy. Is it dead?' He brushes against a tall weed and seeds fall from it onto the dog's fur. I take my hand away quickly, irrationally thinking of fleas leaving their dead host. Michael stands looking down at the dead dog. I look up to tell him that it is dead and see that he is crying. The wind is cuffing his hair, blowing it about his face. He cannot answer Christopher's questions.

He hunkers down beside the dog and I hear him saying, 'Fuck it,' again and again. There is not blood, just a string of saliva which has touched on some rocks. He reaches over and undoes the dog's collar, then begins to put rocks on top of the dog. In silence everybody helps. The skin seems mobile when heavy stones are placed on it. Eventually the dog is covered with cairn and we stand back feeling a ridiculous need for prayer. Christopher does not cry out but keeps watching his father, doing everything that he does except cry. As we turn away Michael says, 'You get very attached to a hound,' almost by way of apology for his crying.

On the way back to the car in darkness, we string out, a single file, about ten yards between each of us, coming together only to help one another over fences.

Father and Son

Because I do not sleep well I hear my father rising to go to work. I know that in a few minutes he will come in to look at me sleeping. He will want to check that I came home last night. He will stand in his bare feet, his shoes and socks in hand, looking at me. I will sleep for him. Downstairs I hear the snap of the switch on the kettle. I hear him not eating anything, going about the kitchen with a stomach full of wind. He will come again to look at me before he goes out to work. He will want a conversation. He climbs the stairs and stands breathing through his nose with an empty lunch box in the crook of his arm, looking at me.

This is my son who let me down. I love him so much it hurts but he won't talk to me. He tells me nothing. I hear him groan and see his eyes flicker open. When he sees me he turns away, a heave of bedclothes in his wake.

'Wake up, son. I'm away to my work. Where are you going today?'
    'What's it to you?'
    'If I know what you're doing I don't worry as much.'
    'Shit.'
I do not sleep. My father does not sleep. The sound of ambulances criss-crosses the dark. I sleep with the daylight. It is safe. At night I hear his bare feet click as he lifts them, walking the lino. The front door shudders as he leaves.

My son is breaking my heart. It is already broken. Is it my fault there is no woman in the house? Is it my fault a good woman should die? His face was never softer than when after I had shaved. A baby pressed to my shaved cheek. Now his chin is sandpaper. He is a man. When he was a boy I took him fishing. I taught him how to tie a blood-knot, how to cast a fly, how to strike so the fish would not escape. How to play a fish. The green bus to quiet days in Toome. Him pestering me with questions. If I leave him alone he will break my heart anyway. I must speak to him. Tonight at tea. If he is in.

'You should be in your bed. A man of your age. It's past one.'

'Let me make you some tea.'

The boy shrugs and sits down. He takes up the paper between him and his father.

'What do you be doing out to this time?'

'Not again.'

'Answer me.'

'Talking.'

'Who with?'

'Friends. Just go to bed, Da, will you?'

'What do you talk about?'

'Nothing much.'

'Talk to me, son.'

'What about?'

My son, he looks confused. I want you to talk to me the way I hear you talk to people at the door. I want to hear you laugh with me like you used to. I want to know what you think. I want to know why you do not eat more. No more than pickings for four weeks. Your face is thin. Your fingers, orange with nicotine. I pulled you away from death once and now you will not talk to me. I want to know if you are in danger again.

'About. . .'

'You haven't shaved yet.'

'I'm just going to. The water in the kettle is hot.'

'Why do you shave at night?'

'Because in the morning my hand shakes.'

58

Your hand shakes in the morning, Da, because you're a coward. You think the world is waiting round the corner to blow your head off. A breakfast of two Valium and the rest of them rattling in your pocket, walking down the street to your work. Won't answer the door without looking out the bedroom window first. He's scared of his own shadow.

Son, you are living on borrowed time. Your hand shook when you got home. I have given you the life you now have. I fed you soup from a spoon when your own hand would have spilled it. Let me put my arm around your shoulders and let me listen to what is making you thin. At the weekend I will talk to him.

It is hard to tell if his bed has been slept in. It is always rumpled. I have not seen my son for two days. Then, on the radio, I hear he is dead. They give out his description. I drink milk. I cry.

But he comes in for his tea.

'Why don't you tell me where you are?'
'Because I never know where I am.'

My mother is dead but I have another one in her place. He is an old woman. He has been crying. I know he prays for me all the time. He used to dig the garden, grow vegetables and flowers for half the street. He used to fish. To take me fishing. Now he just waits. He sits and waits for me and the weeds have taken over. I would like to slap his face and make a man out of him.

'I let you go once — and look what happened.'
'Not this again.'
The boy curls his lip as if snagged on a fish-hook.

For two years I never heard a scrape from you. I read of London in the papers. Watched scenes from London on the news, looking over the reporter's shoulder at people walking in the street. I know you, son, you are easily led. Then a doctor phoned for me at work. The poshest man I ever spoke to.

'I had to go and collect you. Like a dog.'

The boy had taken up a paper. He turns the pages noisily, crackling like fire.

'A new rig-out from Littlewoods.'

Socks, drawers, shirt, the lot. In a carrier bag. The doctor said he had to burn what was on you. I made you have your girl's hair cut. It was Belfast before we spoke. You had the taint of England in your voice.

'Today I thought you were dead.'

Every day you think I am dead. you live in fear. Of your own death. Peeping behind curtains, the radio always loud enough to drown any noise that might frighten you, double locking doors. When you think I am not looking you hold your stomach. You undress in the dark for fear of your shadow falling on the window-blind. At night you lie with the pillow over your head. By your bed a hatchet which you pretend to have forgotten to tidy away. Mice have more courage.

'Well I'm not dead.'

'Why don't you tell me where you go?'

'Look, Da, I have not touched the stuff since I came back. Right?'

'Why don't you have a girl like everybody else?'

'Oh fuck.'

He bundles the paper and hurls it in the corner and stamps up the stairs to his room. The old man shouts at the closed door.

'Go and wash you mouth out.'

He cries again, staring at the ceiling so that the tears run down to his ears.

My son, he is full of hatred. For me, for everything. He spits when he speaks. When he shouts his voice breaks high and he is like a woman. He grinds his teeth and his skin goes white about his mouth. His hands shake. All because I ask him where he goes. Perhaps I need to show him more love. Care for him more than I do.

I mount the stairs quietly to apologise. My son, I am sorry. I do it because I love you. Let me put my arm around you

60

and talk like we used to on the bus from Toome. Why do you fight away from me?

The door swings open and he pushes a hand-gun beneath the pillow. Seen long enough, black and squat, dull like a garden slug. He sits, my son, his hands idling empty, staring hatred.

'Why do you always spy on me, you nosey old bastard?' His voice breaks, his eyes bulge.

'What's that? Under your pillow?

'It's none of your fucking business.'

He kicks the door closed in my face with his bare foot.

I am in the dark of the landing. I must pray for him. On my bended knees I will pray for him to be safe. Perhaps I did not see what I saw. Maybe I am mistaken. My son rides pillion on a motor-bike. Tonight I will not sleep. I do not think I will sleep again.

It is ten o'clock. The news begins. Like a woman I stand drying a plate, watching the headlines. There is a ring at the door. The boy answers it, his shirt-tail out. Voices in the hallway.

My son with friends. Talking. What he does not do with me.

There is a bang. A dish-cloth drops from my hand and I run to the kitchen door. Not believing, I look into the hallway. There is a strange smell. My son is lying on the floor, his head on the bottom stair, his feet on the threshold. The news has come to my door. The house is open to the night. There is no one else. I go to him with damp hands.

'Are you hurt?'

Blood is spilling from his nose.

They have punched you and you are not badly hurt. Your nose is bleeding. Something cold at the back of your neck.

I take my son's limp head in my hands and see a hole in his nose that should not be there. At the base of his nostril.

My son, let my put my arms around you.

61

The Beginnings of a Sin

I believe he's late again thought Colum. He took a clean
white surplice from his bag and slipped it over his head,
steadying his glasses as he did so. It was five to eight. He
sat on the bench and changed his shoes for a black pair of
gutties. Father Lynch said that all his altar-boys must move
as quietly as shadows. When he was late he was usually
in his worst mood. Sometimes he did not turn up at all
and Miss Grant, the housekeeper, would come over and
announce from the back of the church that Father Lynch
was ill and that there would be no Mass that day.

At two minutes to eight Colum heard his footstep at the
vestry door. Father Lynch came in and nodded to the boy.
Colum had never seen anyone with such a sleep-crumpled
face in the mornings. It reminded him of a bloodhound,
there was such a floppiness about his deeply wrinkled skin.
His whole face sagged and sloped into lines of sadness. His
black hair was parted low to the side and combed flat with
Brylcreem. Colum thought his neat hair looked out of place
on top of the disorder of his features.

'Is everything ready?' Father Lynch asked him.

'Yes, Father.'

Colum watched him as he prepared to say Mass. He
began by putting on the amice, like a handkerchief with
strings, at the back of his neck. Next a white alb like
a shroud, reaching to the floor. The polished toe-caps of
his everyday shoes peeped out from underneath. He put
the cincture about his waist and knotted it quickly. He
kissed the embroidered cross on his emerald stole and

hung it round his neck. Lastly he put on the chasuble, very carefully inserting his head through the neck-hole. Colum couldn't make up his mind whether he did not want to stain the vestments with hair-oil or wreck his hair. The chasuble was emerald green with yellow lines. Colum liked the feasts of the martyrs best, with their bright blood colour. Father Lynch turned to him.

'What are you staring at?'

'Nothing, Father.'

'You look like a wee owl.'

'Sorry.'

'Let's get this show on the road,' Father Lynch said, his face still like a sad bloodhound. 'We're late already.'

None of the other altar-boys liked Father Lynch. When they did something wrong, he never scolded them with words but instead would nip them on the upper arm. They said he was too quiet and you could never trust anybody like that. Colum found that he was not so quiet if you asked him questions. He seemed to like Colum better than the others, at least Colum thought so. One day he had asked him why a priest wore so much to say Mass and Father Lynch had spoken to him for about ten minutes, keeping him late for school.

'Normally when people wear beautiful things it is to make their personality stand out. With a priest it is the opposite. He wears so much to hide himself. And the higher up the Church you go, the more you have to wear. Think of the poor Pope with all that trumphery on him.'

After Mass Father Lynch asked him how the ballot tickets were going.

'Great. I've sold —'

'Don't tell me. Keep it as a surprise.'

In the darkness Colum stood at the door waiting. He had rolled up a white ballot ticket and was smoking it, watching his breath cloud the icy air. He pulled his socks up as high as he could to try and keep his legs warm. There was a funny smell from the house, like sour food. The woman came back out with her purse. She was still chewing something.

'What's it in aid of?'

'St Kieran's Church Building Fund.'

'How much are they?'

'Threepence each.'

The woman hesitated, poking about in her purse with her index finger. He told her that the big prize was a Christmas hamper. There was a second prize of whiskey and sherry. She took four tickets, finishing his last book.

'Father Lynch'll not be wanting to win it outright, then.'

He was writing her name on the stubs with his fountain pen.

'Pardon?'

'You're a neat wee writer,' she said. He tore the tickets down the perforations and gave them to her. She handed him a shilling, which he dropped into his jacket pocket. It was swinging heavy with coins.

'There's the snow coming on now,' said the woman, waiting to close the front door. He ran the whole way home holding on to the outside of his pocket. In the house he dried his hair and wiped the speckles of melted snow from his glasses. Two of his older brothers, Rory and Dermot, were sitting on the sofa doing homework balanced on their knees and when he told them it was snowing they ran out to see if it was lying.

He took down his tin and spilled it and the money from his pocket on to the table. He added it all together and counted the number of books of stubs. For each book sold the seller was allowed to keep sixpence for himself. Over the past weeks Colum had sold forty-two books around the doors. He took a pound note and a shilling and slipped them into his pocket. He had never had so much money in his life and there was still a full week to sell tickets before the ballot was drawn.

His mother stood at the range making soda farls on a griddle. When they were cooked they filled the house with their smell and made a dry scuffling noise as he handled them. He heard the front door close and Michael shout 'Hello'. At eighteen he was the eldest and the only wage earner in the house.

'Come on, Colum,' said his mother. 'Clear that table. The hungry working man is in.'

After tea they always said the Family Rosary. Colum would half kneel, half crouch at the armchair with his face almost touching the seat. The cushion smelt of cloth and human. He tried to say the Rosary as best he could, thinking of the Sacred Mysteries while his mouth said the words. He was disturbed one night to see Michael kneeling at the sofa saying the prayers with the Sunday paper between his elbows. Colum counted off the Hail Marys, feeding his shiny lilac rosary beads between his finger and thumb. They were really more suitable for a woman but they had come all the way from Lourdes. Where the loop of the beads joined was a little silver heart with a bubble of Lourdes water in it — like the spirit level in his brother's took kit.

When it came to his turn to give out the prayer Colum always waited until the response was finished — not like his brothers who charged on, overlapping the prayer and the response, slurring their words to get it finished as quickly as possible. They became annoyed with him afterwards, in whispers, accused him of being 'a creeping Jesus'.

At the end of each Rosary their mother said a special prayer 'for the happy Repose of the Soul of Daddy'. Although he had been dead two years, it still brought a lump to Colum's throat. It wouldn't have been so bad if she had said father or something but the word Daddy made him want to cry. Sometimes he had to go on kneeling when the others had risen to their feet in case they should see his eyes.

It was Colum's turn to do the dishes. They had their turns written up on a piece of paper so that there would be no argument. He poured some hot water into the basin from the kettle on the range. It had gone slightly brown from heating. He didn't like the look of it as much as the cold water from the pump. In the white enamel bucket under the scullery bench it looked pure and cool and still. Where the enamel had chipped off, the bucket was blue-black. If you put your hand in the water the fingers seemed to go flat.

He dipped a cup into the basin, rinsed it out and set it on the table. Father Lynch had funny fingers. He had tiny tufts of black hair on the back of each of them. They made Colum feel strange as he poured water from a cruet on to them. The priest would join his trembling index fingers and thumbs and hold them over the glass bowl, then he would take the linen cloth ironed into its folds and wipe them dry. He would put it back in its creases and lay it on Colum's arm. He had some whispered prayers to say when he was doing that. Colum always wondered why Father Lynch was so nervous saying his morning Mass. He had served for others and they didn't tremble like that. Perhaps it was because he was holier than them, that they weren't as much in awe of the Blessed Sacrament as he was. What a frightening thing it must be, to hold Christ's actual flesh — to have the responsibility to change the bread and wine into the body and blood of Jesus.

He dried the dishes and set them in neat piles before putting them back on the shelf. Above the bench Michael had fixed a small mirror for shaving. Colum had to stand on tip-toe to see himself. He was the only one of the family who had to wear glasses. He took after his father. For a long time he had to wear National Health round ones with the springy legs that hooked behind his ears, but after months of pleading and crying his mother had given in and bought him a good pair with real frames.

He went to the back door and threw out a basinful of water with a slap on to the icy ground. It steamed in the light from the scullery window. It was a still night and he could hear the children's voices yelling from the next street.

The kitchen was warm when he came back in again. Radio Luxembourg was on the wireless. Colum took all his money in his pocket and put the stubs in a brown paper bag.

'I'm away, Mammy,' he said.

She was having a cigarette, sitting with her feet up on a stool.

'Don't be late,' was all she said.

He walked a lamp post, ran a lamp post through the town until he reached the hill which led to the Parochial House. It was a large building made of the same red brick as the church. He could see lights on in the house so he climbed the hill. It was still bitterly cold and he was aware of his jaw shivering. He kept both hands in his pockets, holding the brown bag in the crook of his arm. He knocked at the door of the house. It was the priest's housekeeper who opened it a fraction. When she saw Colum she opened it wide.

'Hello, Miss Grant. Is Father Lynch in?'

'He is busy, Colum. What was it you wanted?'

'Ballot tickets, Miss. And to give in money.'

She looked over her shoulder down the hallway, then turned and put out her hand for the money.

'It's all loose, Miss,' said Colum, digging into his pocket to let her hear it.

'Oh, you'd best come in then — for a moment.'

Miss Grant brought him down the carpeted hallway to her quarters — she had a flat of her own at the back of the house. She closed the door and smiled a jumpy kind of smile — a smile that stopped in the middle. Colum emptied the bag of stubs on the table.

'There's forty-two books. . .' he said.

'Goodness, someone has been busy.'

'. . . and here is five pounds, five shillings.' He set two pound notes and a ten shilling note on the table and hand-fulled the rest of the coins out of his pocket. They rang and clattered on the whitewood surface. She began to check it, scraping the coins towards her quickly and building them into piles.

'All present and correct,' she said.

Colum looked at the sideboard. There was a bottle of orange juice and a big box of biscuits which he knew was for the ticket sellers. She saw him looking.

'All right, all right,' she said.

She poured a glass of juice and allowed him to choose two biscuits. His fingers hovered over the selection.

'Oh come on, Colum, don't take all night.'

He took a chocolate one and a wafer and sat down. He had never seen Miss Grant so snappy before. Usually she was easygoing. She was very fat, with a chest like stuffed pillows under her apron. He had heard the grown-ups in the town say that if anybody had earned heaven it was her. They spoke of her goodness and kindness. 'There's one saint

67

in that Parochial House,' they would say. For a long time Column thought they were talking about Father Lynch.

In the silence he heard his teeth crunching the biscuit. Miss Grant did not sit down but stood by the table waiting for him to finish. He swallowed and said,

'Could I have ten more books, please?'

'Yes, dear.' She put her hands in her apron pocket and looked all around her, then left the room.

Colum had never been in this part of the house before. He had always gone into Father Lynch's room or waited in the hallway. Although it was a modern house, it was full of old things. A picture of the Assumption of Our Lady in a frame of gold leaves hung by the front door. The furniture in Father Lynch's room was black and heavy. The dining room chairs had twisted legs like barley sugar sticks. Everything had a rich feel to it, especially the thick patterned carpet. Miss Grant's quarters were not carpeted but had some rugs laid on the red tiled floor. It was the kind of floor they had at home, except that the corners of their tiles were chipped off and they had become uneven enough to trip people.

'Vera!' he heard a voice shout. It was Father Lynch.

Vera's voice answered from somewhere. Colum looked up and Father Lynch was standing in the doorway with his arm propped against the jamb.

'Hello, Father.'

'Well, if it isn't the owl,' said Father Lynch.

He wasn't dressed like a priest but was wearing an ordinary man's collarless shirt, open at the neck.

'What brings you up here, Colum?'

He moved from the door and reached out to put his hand on a chair back. Two strands of his oiled hair had come loose and fallen over his forehead. He sat down very slowly on the chair.

'Ballot tickets, Father. I've sold all you gave me.'

Father Lynch gave a loud whoop and slapped the table loudly with the flat of his hand. His eyes looked very heavy and he was blinking a lot.

'That's the way to do it. Lord, how the money rolls in.'

He was slurring his words as if he was saying the Rosary. Miss Grant came into the room holding a wad of white ballot tickets.

'Here you are now, Colum. You'd best be off.'

Colum finished his juice and stood up.

'Is that the strongest you can find for the boy to drink, Vera?' He laughed loudly. Colum had never heard him laugh before. He slapped the table again.

'Father — if you'll excuse us, I'll just show Colum out now.'

'No. No. He came to see me — didn't you?'

Colum nodded.

'He's the only one that would. Let him stay for a bit.'

'His mother will worry about him.'

'No she won't,' said Colum.

'Of course she won't,' said Father Lynch. He ignored Miss Grant. 'How many books did you sell?'

'Forty-two, Father.'

The priest raised his eyes to heaven and blew out his cheeks. Colum smelt a smell like altar wine.

'Holy Saint Christopher. Forty-two?'

'Yes.'

Miss Grant moved behind Colum and began to guide him with pressure away from the table.

'That calls for a celebration.' Father Lynch stood up unsteadily. 'Forty-two!'

He reached out to give Colum a friendly cuff on the back of the head but he missed and instead his hand struck the side of the boy's face scattering his glasses on the tiled floor.

'Aw Jesus,' said the priest. 'I'm sorry.' Father Lynch hunkered down to pick them up but lurched forward on to his knees. One lens was starred with white and the arc of the frame was broken. He hoisted himself to his feet and held the glasses close to his sagging face, looking at them.

'Jesus, I'm so sorry,' he said again. He bent down, looking for the missing piece of frame, and the weight of his head seemed to topple him. He cracked his skull with a sickening thump off the sharp edge of a radiator. One of his legs was still up in the air trying to right his balance. He put his hand to the top of his head and Colum saw that the hand was slippery with blood. Red blood was smeared from his Brylcreemed hair on to the radiator panel as the priest slid lower. His eyes were open but not seeing.

'Are you all right, Father?' Miss Grant's voice was shaking. She produced a white handkerchief from her apron pocket. The priest shouted, his voice suppressed and hissing and angry. He cursed his housekeeper and the polish on her floor. Then he raised his eyes to her without moving his head and said in an ordinary voice, 'What a mess for the boy.'

Miss Grant took the glasses which he was still clutching and put them in Colum's hand. Father Lynch began to cry with his mouth half open. Miss Grant turned the boy away and pushed him towards the door. Both she and Colum had to step over the priest to get out. She led him by the elbow down the hallway.

'That's the boy. Here's your ballot tickets.'

She opened the front door.

'Say a wee prayer for him, Colum. He's in bad need of it.'

'All right, but —'

'I'd better go back to him now.'

The door closed with a slam. Colum put his glasses on but could only see through his left eye. His knees were like water and his stomach was full of wind. He tried to get some of it up but he couldn't. He started to run. He ran all the way home. He sat panting on the cold doorstep and only went in when he got his breath back. His mother was alone.

'What happened to you? You're as white as a sheet,' she said, looking up at him. She was knitting a grey sock on three needles shaped into a triangle. Colum produced his glasses from his pocket. Within the safety of the house he began to cry.

'I bust them.'

'How, might I ask?' His mother's voice was angry.

'I was running and they just fell off. I slipped on the ice.'

'Good God, Colum, do you know how much those things cost? You'll have to get a new pair for school. Where do you think the money is going to come from? Who do you think I am, Carnegie? Eh?'

Her knitting needles were flashing and clacking. Colum continued to cry, tears rather than noise.

'Sheer carelessness. I've a good mind to give you a thumping.'

Colum, keeping out of range of her hand, sat at the table and put the glasses on. He could only half see. He put his hand in his pocket and took out his pound note.

'Here,' he said offering it to his mother. She took it and put it beneath the jug on the shelf.

'That'll not be enough,' she said, then after a while, 'Will you stop that sobbing? It's not the end of the world.'

The next morning Colum was surprised to see Father Lynch in the vestry before him. He was robed and reading his breviary, pacing the strip of carpet in the centre of the room. They said nothing to each other.

At the Consecration Colum looked up and saw the black congealed wound on the thinning crown of Father Lynch's head, as he lifted the tail of the chasuble. He saw him elevate the white disc of the host and heard him mutter the words, '*Hoc est enim corpus meum.*'

Colum jangled the cluster of bells with angry twists of his wrist. A moment later when the priest raised the chalice full of wine he rang the bell again, louder if possible.

In the vestry afterwards he changed as quickly as he could and was about to dash out when Father Lynch called him. He had taken off his chasuble and was folding it away.

'Colum.'

'What?'

'Sit down a moment.'

He removed the cincture and put it like a coiled snake in the drawer. The boy remained standing. The priest sat down in his alb and beckoned him over.

'I'm sorry about your glasses.'

Colum stayed at the door and Father Lynch went over to him. Colum thought his face no longer sad, simply ugly.

'Your lace is loosed.' He was about to genuflect to tie it for him but Colum crouched and tied it himself. Their heads almost collided.

'It's hard for me to explain,' said Father Lynch, 'but. . .to a boy of your age sin is a simple thing. It's not.'

Colum smelt the priest's breath sour and sick.

'Yes, Father.'

'That's because you have never committed a sin. You don't know about it.'

He removed his alb and hung it in the wardrobe.

'Trying to find the beginnings of a sin is like. . .' He looked at the boy's face and stopped. 'Sin is a deliberate turning away from God. That is an extremely difficult thing to do. To close Him out from your love. . .'

'I'll be late for school, Father.'

'I suppose you need new glasses?'

'Yes.'

Father Lynch put his hand in his pocket and gave him some folded pound notes.

'Did you mention it to your mother?'

'What?'

'How they were broken?'

'No.'

'Are you sure? To anyone?'

Colum nodded that he hadn't. He was turning to get out the door. The priest raised his voice, trying to keep him there.

'I knew your father well, Colum,' he shouted. 'You remind me of him a lot.'

The altar-boy ran, slamming the door after him. He heard an empty wooden coat-hanger rattle on the hardboard panel of the door and it rattled in his mind until he reached the bottom of the hill. There he stopped running. He unfolded the wad of pound notes still in his hand and counted one — two — three — four of them with growing disbelief.

The Deep End

On the way home in the empty bus the two boys were silent. They sat as usual in separate seats but made no attempt to avoid paying their fare. Paul sat, his damp towel clenched in the crook of his arm, looking down into the street at each stop. At Manor Street Olly knelt up and looked back at him.

'Say nothing to your Ma, for God's sake, Paul. We'd never get going again.'

'I'm not mad about going again — not for a while,' said Paul.

Olly unfurled his bundle and took out his togs and wrung them out, the droplets splashing onto the battened floor.

'Where are you for this afternoon?' he asked.

'Any dough?'

'Naw.' Olly got up and ran down the bus. 'See ya,' he shouted. Halfway down the stairs he stopped and pulled a cigarette out of his top pocket.

'I'll smoke your half for you, Paul.'

'I hope it chokes you,' Paul called after him.

Paul went home and couldn't eat his dinner. He went up to the bedroom and lay for a long time looking at the ceiling. His mother came up and put her head round the door.

'That's the last time you'll go to the baths — your guts full of oul' lime water — and God knows what else. I'm sure they do more than swim in the water.'

Paul suddenly felt his eyes fill with tears. Then he cried hard. His mother came over and put her arms round him, asking incredulously, 'What's wrong, what's wrong with my big man?'

They queued in the hallway and heard the distant echoing cease. Above them, on the wall, was an Artificial Respiration poster, its reds gone brown in the sun. Dotted lines and arrows showed the right motions. Somebody had drawn tits on the victim's back and added genitals to the man bending over him. Olly stood, one foot flat against the cream tiled wall, the other slanted like a prop.

'Away and ask her how long they'll be,' he said. Paul crushed his way up to the porthole and came back.

'Ten minutes.'

'Time for a feg.' With two fingers Olly dipped into his breast pocket and pulled out a cigarette. He straightened it out and tapped the loose tobacco into place on his thumb nail. 'Smoke one now and the other one after.'

Paul struck the match between the tiles. Olly cupped the flame in his hands, took two quick puffs then closed his fingers round the cigarette. He leaned back against the wall.

'Don't suck the guts out of it.' Olly turned his head away from Paul's reaching hand, taking the last ounce out of it.

'Come on, it'll be red hot,' said Paul grabbing the cigarette from him. He couldn't inhale as deeply as Olly so he blew the smoke down his nose and passed it back.

'What are they?' he asked.

'Parkies,' said Olly.

'They're OK'. Then after a moment Paul asked, 'Do you believe this cancer thing?'

'Naw, sure my Ma and Da both smoke like trains and look at the age they are.'

'Oul' Hennesy smoked and he's dead — fifty a day,' said Paul.

'You've gotta go sometime — where the hell did oul' Hennesy get the money. Fifty a day. Jesis.'

'All the doctors say it,' said Paul.

'Doctors are stupid. My Da was walking around for two weeks with a broken finger and they didn't even know. They had to send him to the hospital before they found out.' Olly tucked in the loose strands of tobacco at the soggy end with his finger.

'Does your Ma still not allow you?' he asked.

'Naw.'

'Mine gave me one yesterday — she said as long as nobody was in it was OK. She says it's better than smoking behind her back.'

'My Ma would do her nut if she knew.'

A small boy nudged Olly and, looking up at him, said, 'Give us your butt.'

'Fuck off, son,' said Olly dropping the remains of the cigarette on the ground and pressing it with a twist of his toe.

'What about clubbing up for currant squares when we get out?' Paul asked.

'From Lizzie's?'

'Yeah, they're dead on.'

'OK,' said Olly. 'How much have we?'

They took out their money and calculated. If bus fares weren't collected that was so much profit, but a keen conductor had to be allowed for. They had enough. Paul licked his lips and growled.

By now the first crowd had begun to come out in ones and twos. White faced, red eyed, some with their togs on their heads, others their hair wet and spiky, they tumbled out, shouting at each other at the tops of their voices. One boy in raggy jeans, both elbows out of his sweater climbed to the top of the turnstile gate, almost to the ceiling and slopped his wet togs down onto the back of his friend's neck.

'Get to hell out of it,' roared the attendant who had just come out. He stood threatening, his fingers hooked in the loops of his belt, brown muscled in a singlet and jeans. He wore black wellingtons with the white canvas rims turned down. He had a tattoo, blue and red on each arm. The boy scuttled down off the gate and crashed out the door. The attendant said something to the girl behind the pay box and the line began to jostle and fight to get through.

Paul shoved his way up to the arched hole in the perspex and pushed his money to the girl. She gave him a ticket, a towel and a pair of trunks. The towel was a freshly laundered dishcloth, still warm with a clean smell, the trunks a double red triangle held together with string. Paul used the Corporation towel for standing on and dried himself with his own soft towel. The gym teacher had told them the worst thing you could get out of the baths was athletes foot and he himself stood on a towel. Paul's mother always harped on about polio.

'If you had to spend the rest of your days in a wheel-chair it would be a dear swim. The ones that swim over there, you never know what homes they've come out of. It's a bad area.'

'But the water's full of chlorine, Ma.'

'Chlorine, chlorine — what's the use of chlorine if you're going to get polio. Eh? Tell me that. Your father's too soft, allowing you. He says the swimming'll make a man out of you but he'll change his tune if it makes a polio victim out of you.'

Both boys ran down the corridor, their heels hollow yet pinging from the ceiling. They raced through the swing doors looking beneath each half door for a box without a pair of feet. They each got a box to themselves at the deep end. Paul climbed up onto the seat so that he could see out as he got stripped. The pool still moved from the previous session. It looked still enough on the surface but the black lane lines snaked to and fro continuously. He hauled off his pullover, shirt and vest as one unit and hung them on the peg. The same with his trousers and drawers. The whole lot hung like somebody deformed, humped with dangling arms.

Suddenly there was a cry smothered by a dull explosion. Paul looked out over the partition and saw a boy at the bottom of his dive, alone in the pool. He looked flat, spread-eagled, his hair middle shaded and smoothed by the water. He breast-stroked to the surface and blew out a farting noise.

'First in.' It was Olly. 'Get a move on, Paul,' he screamed.

Paul hopped about on one leg putting on his black trunks. Then he put the Corporation ones over them, tying the string at the sides. The red and black looked nice. If you *only* wore the Corporation ones your thing kept showing.

He blessed himself, said the first line of an Act of Contrition and went out of the box. He walked jerkily down to the three foot end, holding his elbows. The water splashed out on the sides and was cold underfoot. By now the pool was threshing with swimmers and the noise was deafening.

'Look at the ribs,' screamed Olly's head.

Paul moved down the steps at the three foot mark and stood on the last step, knee deep.

He splashed some water over his shoulders and face. Then he pushed himself off from the side screaming with cold. Paul had just learned to swim. He could breast-stroke a breadth at the shallow end but above four feet he kept close to the bar. Somebody had once told him, 'If you can swim a breadth you can swim a mile,' but he didn't believe it. He stood for a while jumping up and down stirring the water with his hands. Olly swam down to him and they played diving between each other's legs for a while. Then Olly headed off for the high board. Paul half swam, half pulled himself along the bar to the deep end. Olly climbed the steps to the top board, swiping the wet hair from his eyes. Paul treaded water waiting and watching him. When he reached the top he held onto the railing, a boxer in his corner, then ran and launched himself into the air, his heels cocked and fifteen foot down, exploded into the water. He came up beside Paul.

'Come on and try,' he said. 'It's great.'

'Are you mad?'

'You're yella. Once you've done it once, it's dead easy. Come on.' He swam to the steps and Paul followed. They sloshed out of the water and began climbing the ladder. At the top Paul looked down at the squat, upturned faces and held tight to the rail.

'Ready?' Olly asked.

'You go first.'

'Go on, I want to watch you.'

'You go first or I won't go,' said Paul.

Olly ran and disappeared at the end of the wet matting on the board, plummeting out of sight. Paul blessed himself and waited until Olly came up again.

'Are you yella?' He laughed appearing up the ladder. He ran past Paul and jumped again holding his nose. Paul let go the bar and scrambled quickly down the ladder and jumped as high as he could off the side of the pool. The bubbles seethed up his nose and his ears pounded and rumbled. He came up near Olly.

'I did it,' he shouted.

Olly swam over to him and said, 'Good for you. I thought you were chicken. Come on again.'

'Naw,' said Paul. 'Once is enough. What about playing tig?'

But the tig was no use because Olly would dive into the middle of the six foot end and couldn't be caught.

Afterwards Paul stood out on the side to get his breath back. The sour taste of the lime made him wish for his currant square now. It was colder out of the water than in. Goose pimples came out all over his body and the light hairs on his arms stood up. 'You could strike matches on ye,' his father had once said to him at the sea-side. 'It couldn't be good for him,' his mother added, huddled in the depths of her deck chair. Paul stood shivering and listening to the din. Splashing and slamming of dressing box doors mixed with a continuous jagged scream, which echoed and multiplied when flung back from the high glass roof. It started at the beginning of the session and stayed at the same sawing pitch throughout. The long whistle to end the session shrilled and the noise reached a crescendo as everybody plunged in for the last time.

Paul was near his box and felt too cold for a last fling. He pushed the half door shut and spread the cotton towel on the duck-boarding. He began to dry himself slowly. He peeled off his trunks and left them, a wet figure eight, at his feet. He felt alone in the box. The noise was outside, people whistling, shouting jokes, but inside he was safe and insulated. Private. He looked down at himself, at his wisps of hair. He wondered if he would ever have a bush like the gym teachers. 'You're on the verge of life now my dear boys — soon you will become men,' the Redemptorist, his black and white heart pinned to his chest, smiled. 'And I know you will all make very good men — every last one of you.' Paul dried himself and pulled on his drawers trying not to think about it any more. Then suddenly from outside there was a scream, totally different in tone from any of the shouting and larking that was going on.

'*Hey mister, mister.*'

Paul stood up on the seat and looked out. A boy, half-dressed, was running up and down the side of the pool pointing into it and screaming all the time, *'mister, mister.'* Paul looked and saw a still figure lying on the bottom at the deep end. The attendant raced past his box and plunged in. He scooped the body up off the bottom and swam with it to the side. Another man took it from him, by an arm and a leg. The boy's mouth was black and open. Paul sat down on the seat so he couldn't see. Everything was completely silent now except for one of the boys who was snivelling and crying. Paul dried his feet and put on his socks. He pulled on his trousers and stood up to look out again. In the middle of a quiet crowd of boys the attendant was kneeling, his clothes darkened with the wet. The boy's body was blue-grey and when the attendant did anything with its arms, they flopped. Paul stood down and finished dressing. He whispered over to Olly, 'Will we go?'

'Wait t'see what happens.' Olly, in his vest, hung over the half door.

'Is he dead?' Paul hissed.

'Looks like it,' said Olly.

Paul sat down again. The box was painted dark green. Initials and dates, crude guitar shapes of women with split and tits were carved or drawn on every square inch of space. He began to read them — 'G.B. WUZ HERE' — TONY IS A WANKER' — 'BMcK 1955.' He read these things over and over again until in the distance he heard the bray of an ambulance. It drew close and stopped. There were some sweet papers and a few dead matches lodged beneath the struts of the duck-boards at his feet. He picked up his togs and very slowly disentangled them from the red ones. Olly came in dressed.

'What's happening?' Paul asked.

'They're away.'

Paul looked out. The crowd had gone and everyone was back in their boxes getting dressed. Someone started to whistle but stopped. The pool was absolutely still now, the black lines at the bottom ruled rigid, perspective straight, the surface a turquoise pane.

They walked straddle-legged down the slippery edge of the pool and threw their borrowed togs and towels into the bin. Outside at the turnstile the girl had put a piece of cardboard over the porthole and there was a queue, quieter than usual, waiting to see if they were going to get in or not.

The boys walked down the steps and crossed the road to the bus stop at Lizzie's bakery. Olly looked at the currant squares in the window. About a quarter of a trayful had been sold. Then he too leaned his back against the window and the two of them stood, their heads turned, waiting for a bus.

My Dear Palestrina

'Come on, love, it's for your own good,' she said. Rooks from
the trees above set up a slow, raucous cawing. Cinders had
spilled on the footpath and they cracked and spat beneath
their shoes, echoing in the arch of the trees overhead, as
they walked the mile from the town to Miss Schwartz's
place. The boy stayed one pace behind and slightly to the left
of his mother. To show her determination, she had begun by
taking his hand but it seemed foolish to be seen dragging a
boy of his age. Although now they were separate they were
so far gone along the road that she knew she had won. The
boy stopped at the old forge and stared at the door into
the dark, listening to the high pinging of the blacksmith's
hammer.

'Don't have me to go back, Danny, or I'll make an example
of you.' She waited, looking over her shoulder at him. His
eyes were still red from crying.

Miss Schwartz had a beautifully polished brass knocker
on her black front door. It resounded deep within the house.
It seemed a long time before she answered. When she did, it
was with politeness.

'Yes, can I help you?'

The boy's mother smiled back and nodded down the path
to where the boy was standing.

'I want him to have piana lessons,' she said.

Mrs McErlane, panting after the walk, fell into an
armchair, propped her bag on her knee and listened as
Miss Schwartz struck single notes for her Danny to sing.
His voice was clear but not rich and still had reverberations

81

of the long afternoon's crying in it. Her long pale finger poked about the piano and no matter where it went Danny's voice followed it. Then she played clusters of notes and Danny repeated them. She asked the boy to turn away and struck a note.

'Can you find that note?' and Danny played it. She did this again and again and each time the boy found it. At the doorstep on the way out Miss Schwartz said that the pleasure in teaching would be hers. *Auf wiedersehen.*

'Did you hear that?' said Mrs McErlane on the way home. 'Anyway it will be good for you. It's a lovely thing to have. The others is too old to learn now.'

Danny said nothing but hunched his shoulders against the darkness and the cold of the night that was coming on.

'I hated to think of that piana going to waste,' she said.

Because the McErlanes had a boy young enough to learn, it was they who got the piano when Uncle George died. They also got a lawn mower and a vacuum cleaner, even though they had no carpet in the house.

The piano came in the night when Danny was in bed. When he had visited Uncle George, Danny would slip into the front room on his own and climb up on the piano stool and single-finger notes. He liked to play the white ones because afterwards, when he struck a black note it was so sad that it gave him a funny feeling in his tummy. The piano stool had a padded seat which opened. Inside were wads of old sheet music with film stars' pictures on the front.

Bing Crosby, Johnny Ray, Rosemary Clooney. He had heard her singing on the radio.

A cannon-ball don't pay no mind
Whether you're gentle or you're kind.

It was about a civil war. He liked the way she twirled her voice. When he tried to sing that song he always put on an American accent.

Two brothers on their way
One wore blue and one wore grey.

After school he walked to his first lesson on a road that fumed with dry snow and wind. The door of the forge was closed and the place silent. On the way out a car passed him, returning to town. A white face pressed itself up against the back window. White hari, blue glasses and a red tongue sticking out at him. Mingo. Danny hated Mingo, with his strange eyes and white fleshy skin. Some of the boys in school had told him that Mingo was from Albania and they were all like that there.

Miss Schwartz had a warm fire blazing in her front room.

'You must be cold,' she said. 'Come, warm your hands.'

Danny held out his chapped hands and felt the heat on them. He rubbed the warmed palms on his bare knees, trying to thaw them out. Miss Schwartz smiled.

'You are such a good-looking boy,' she said. Danny stood embarrassed, his brown eyes averted, looking down at the fire. His blond hair had been cuffed and ruffled by the wind and gave him a wild look.

'You look like the Angel Gabriel,' she said and pulled her mouth into a wide smile. 'Sit down — near the fire — and let me tell you about music.' She spoke with a strange accent, as if some of her words were squeezed into the wrong shape. Her mouth was elastic. Danny knew every word she said but it was not the way he had heard anybody talk before.

'What kind of music do you like?'

'I dunno,' said Danny after a moment's thought.

'Do you have a favourite singer?'

'I like Elvis.'

'Rubbish,' she said, still smiling. 'What I am going to tell you now you will not believe. You will not understand it, but I have to tell you all the same. I will teach you about things. I hope I will nurture in you a love you will never forget.' The smile had disappeared from her face and her eyes widened and drilled into Danny's. 'Music is the most beautiful thing in the world. Today beautiful is a word that has been dirtied, but I mean it truly. Beautiful.' She let the word hang in the air between them.

'Music is why I do not die. Other people — they have blood put in their arms,' she stabbed a fingernail at the inside of her elbow, 'I am kept alive by music. It is the food of love, as you say. I stress that you will not believe me, but what

83

you *must* do is *trust* me. I will show it to you if you will let me. Rilke says that music begins where speech ends — and he should know.'

Danny looked at her and the two pin-head reflections of the fire in her eyes. She was good-looking, with a long thin face and a broad mouth which she was constantly contorting as she wrestled to make the strange words clear. She did not wear lipstick like his mother. Her jet black hair was pulled back into a knot at the back of her neck and her parting was straight, as if ruled. Danny had seen her from the back when she played the organ in church and occasionally when she had come into the town shops, a dark figure hardly worth notice, her basket on her stiff forearm, her wrist to the sky. But here she seemed to fill the room with her talk and her flashing hands. All the time she sat on the edge of her chair, leaning towards him, talking into him. He swayed back as far as his stool would let him.

'Wait,' she said. She got up and went over to a bureau and took out a sheet of paper from a typewriter. She held it up.

'Look. Look hard at this.'

Danny looked but could see nothing, only the slight curl at the bottom of the page where it had lain in the machine.

'I give you a white sheet of paper. It is nothing. But the black marks. . . The black marks, Danny. That is what makes it important. The music, the words. They are the black marks,' she said, and her whole face blazed with passion. 'I am going to teach you those marks. Then I am going to teach you to make the most wonderful music from them. Come, let us begin.' As she sat down at the piano she snorted. 'Elvis Presley!'

When the lesson was over Miss Schwartz got up and went out, saying that they both deserved a cup of tea. Danny sat on the piano stool and looked at the room. It was a strange place, covered in pictures. Behind the pictures the wallpaper was dark brown, or else so old that it looked dark brown. There were plants in pots standing in saucers all over the place. Large dark green spikes with leathery leaves, small hanging plants, one with a pale flower on it. The wind pressured round the house and buffeted in the chimney. He could hear the ticking of

84

fresh snow on the windows and the drone of a lorry taking the hill.

'I hope it lies,' he said to himself. The fire hissed and blew out a small feather of flame.

Miss Schwartz, carrying a tray, closed the door with her toe, which peeped out from her dressing-gown. It was black silk, long to the floor and hanging loosely about her body. On the back it had a strange Chinese pattern in scarlet and green and silver threads. It reminded Danny of the one the magician wore in the Rupert Bear strip in the *Daily Express*.

'Now, while we drink our tea I will have to play you some music,' she said. She lifted the lid of one of the pieces of furniture and put on a record. She turned it up so loud that the music bulged in the room. Danny had never heard anything like it and he hated it. It had no tune and he kept waiting for somebody to sing but nobody did. He ate two biscuits and drank his tea as quickly as he could. Then she let him go.

On his way home the January wind cut his face and riffled the practice music he carried clenched under his arm. In the telephone wires above he heard the sounds of a peeled privet switch being whipped through the air again and again and again. At the forge he crossed the road to have a closer look. It was more of a shack than a building, with walls made of corrugated iron and hardboard of different faded and peeling colours. Someone had cleaned a paintbrush by the door or had tried out various colours on the wall. The place was surrounded by bits of broken and rusting machinery from farms. From the dark came the rhythmic sound of hammering. Danny edged into the open doorway and it stopped. A man's voice came out of the blackness.

'What do you want, lad?'

Danny jumped.

'C'mere,' said the voice. Danny moved to the threshold, trying to see into the gloom. 'What can I do for you?'

'Just looking.'

'Well, you'll never see from out there. Come in.'

The place smelt of metal and coke fumes and oil. Danny could make out a man in a leather apron. He looked too

85

young to be a blacksmith, with his tight black curly hair.

'What's your name?' he asked. When Danny told him he thought for a moment. 'Your Da's a bus driver? Am I right or am I wrong?'

The man talked as he worked, heating a strip of metal in the coke of his fire and hammering it while it was red. Each hammer blow pulsed through Danny's head like the record at Miss Schwartz's.

'And what has you up this end of town?' Danny told him he was going to music.

'To Miss Warts and all?' he shouted 'I wonder would she like this song?' He began to sing loudly, and bang his hammer to the rhythm, 'If I was a blackbird'. When he came to the line 'And I'd bury my head on her lily white breast', he winked at Danny. He had a good voice and could get twirls into it — like Rosemary Clooney. When he had finished the song, he asked Danny about school. He didn't seem to think much of it because he said it was the worst place to learn anything. He talked a lot and Danny helped him to work the bellows for his fire. When he took the red hot metal out of the fire, it had tiny lights that flashed and disappeared. The man said that that was the dust touching it and burning up. As the smith worked, Danny looked at his arms, not muscled, but tight with sinews and strings, pounding at the metal. He shouted to make himself heard over his work.

'The schools make the people they want. They get rid of their cutting edge. That's how they keep us quiet.' He nodded that he wanted Danny to pump harder. 'It'll not always be like that. Our time will come, boy, and it'll not be horseshoes we'll be beating out. No, sir.'

Danny was breathless with the pumping. The blacksmith looked at him, raising one eyebrow.

'Are you the lad that was very ill not so long ago?'

Danny breathed and nodded.

'Then maybe you better quit and be off home.'

Danny picked up his music from the cluttered bench and blew the brown rust from it. As he left the man shouted after him, 'Just give us a call any time you're passing, son.'

Danny tried to walk the road in step to the fading ring of his hammer.

When he came through the back door his mother yelled at him, 'Where's the good cap I knitted for you?'

'Oh, sorry, I left it behind.'

She began to help him unbutton his coat, scolding with concern.

'You are not strong yet, you know. I don't know what that woman was thinking of, letting you out without it. Are your ears not freezing?'

'I'm O.K.'

'You are not indeed. I never met your equal for catching things. There's not much the doctors don't know about that you haven't had. Twice over maybe. You must look after yourself, Danny.'

The boy went up to his room and lay on the bed. his mother was right. He seemed to be constantly ill. The last time had been the worst. The one nice thing he could remember about it was having the bed made while he was in it. He would lie there while his mother pulled all the bed-clothes off, then she would straighten the sheet beneath him, tugging it with exaggerated grunts. 'The weight of you!' she would say. He would run his fingers fan-like across the smoothness under him. His mother, separating out the clothes and standing at the end of the bed, would flap the upper sheet to make it fall soothingly on top of him. It came slow and cool and milky down over him with a breath of cotton-smelling air. It was almost transparent and he could look down at his feet and see himself in a white world — his tent, his isolation. The light came through, but he was cut off. He made no attempt to take the sheet down from his face. He heard her voice, then felt the heavier blankets fall across his body, the light disappearing. Only then would he turn back the sheet and look at her. He had wanted to remain suspended in the moment of the sheet, in its relaxation and whiteness, but it always came to an end. He knew that he made peaks at his head and at his toes. He had seen furniture covered this way, and his grandfather in the hospital morgue.

'Now sit up for your medicine.' It had been white too. Cloying sweetness trying to disguise a revolting base flavour. His father gave him sixpence if he could keep it down. After a week he had a shilling on his bedside table. His mother opened *her* mouth when she gave him the stuff. She set the spoon down and lifted the bowl in readiness. His tongue furred with the mixture. Little squirts of warm saliva came into his mouth and he gagged but it stayed down. 'Good boy. Another sixpence. Sure, you'll be rich by the end of the bottle.'

Now he rolled off the bed and decided to go downstairs and let his mother hear what he had learned that day.

'First, empty that,' she said. Danny went to the compost heap at the bottom of the garden with the scraps. On the way back he swung the empty colander and listened to the quiet hoot and whine of the wind through its holes. He liked listening to things. In the room with the two clocks he liked to hear how the ticks would catch up with one another, have the same double tick for a moment and then whisper off into two separate ticks again. The hiss of Miss Schwartz's dressing-gown as she moved. The thin squeak of his compass as he opened its legs. The pop his father's lips made when he was lighting his pipe. He left the empty colander on the draining board.

'Are you ready?' he asked her. His mother listened to his scales, her head cocked to one side, drying her hands on her apron. He played them haltingly.

'There's not much of a tune to that,' she said. 'How much do you have to practise?'

'Until I get it right, she says.'

'Who's "she", something the cat brought in?'

'Miss Schwartz.'

'Have a bit of respect, Danny.'

Danny seemed to get it right with little effort, but what little he did he had to be goaded into by his mother. There was nothing Miss Schwartz taught him that he couldn't do after several attempts. So, in the first months, Miss Schwartz increased the level of difficulty and the duration of his practice pieces. And he was always able for them. Along the sides of the lane that led to her house Danny saw the yellow celandine and the white ones with the strange smell. Wild garlic, she had called them. He met Mingo coming down the lane to where his father had parked the car. Mingo made a vulgar noise with his mouth as they passed but Danny ignored him. Miss Schwartz held the door open and he gave her the envelope with the clinking money in it.

Seated at the piano, he asked,

'Is Mingo any good?'

'Mingo?'

'The boy with the white hair that's just left.'

'Is that what you call him? That boy. . .' she paused, 'is average.'

'Is he as good as me?'

'Do not worry about other people. You will go forward as fast as you are able.' She smiled at him the way he looked at her, then added, 'You knew more on your first day than Mingo, as you call him, will in all his life. Now let me hear you play.'

Danny played his piece and when he had finished she shrugged and smiled.

'It is perfect,' she said, 'but still it is mechanical. Danny, you are a little machine. A pianola. Listen.' She sat on the stool and began to play. Danny listened, watching her closed eyes, the almost imperceptible sway of her body as she stroked music from the notes. 'At this point it must sing. *Cantabile.*' She talked over her playing, pointing out to him where he had gone wrong. 'Now try it again.'

Danny played the piece again and when it was over Miss Schwartz's eyes sparkled.

'That was much better,' she said. 'Beautiful. You learn so quickly.'

'I can't play like that at home,' he said, 'but here it's different.'

'I think,' said Miss Schwartz, 'it is time for an examination. It will please your mother. And I think it will please you because we will get a trip to the city. And. . .' she added after more thought, 'it will please me. I will write a note to your mother. Although I will not say this in the letter, if you have any difficulties with the bus fare

89

I will pay it myself. Do not say it, of course, if there are no difficulties.'

They began to work on a new piece by her darling Schubert and when she felt they had accomplished enough she got up and made tea.

Alone in the room, Danny stared at the pictures. Silhouettes, she called them. Jet black outlines of composers she had named. Beethoven, Mahler on the tips of his toes, Schubert. He liked Beethoven the best, the way his hair sprouted in all directions.

As they drank their tea she played again the record that she had played at their first lesson. Now Danny knew it and could hum the melody as it played.

Some weeks ago, when she had come back in with the tea, she had found Danny in the corner, crouched looking at her records. She kept them in a huge set of books, each page with a circular hole in it so that you could see the label of the record. Danny turned the stiff pages of the records, carefully looking at the labels, scarlet ones with a dog barking into a horn, green ones with the title in tilted writing. He took out a record and looked closely at its surface, angling it to the light. Intense black with light shining in the grooves. She handled them like eggs. When she came in all she said was, 'Be careful, Danny.' She poured the tea and then continued her sentence, 'or they will end up like this.' She leaned over and lifted a record which had a large bite out of its side.

'Some boys who come here are not as careful as you. Goodbye, Dinu Lipatti. I think I will have to make a flower-pot out of you. You see?' She pointed to one of her plants. A record had been folded up in some way to make a container 'You heat it and you mould it until it is the shape you want. I hate to waste anything. That's what comes of the war.' She bit into her gingersnap and said through her chewing, 'I would like to stand on his glasses.'

Danny liked to dip his into his tea and bite the warm, mushy sweetness.

When he handed Miss Schwartz's note to his mother, she ruffled his hair with her hand.

'You're losing your blondness,' she said, 'but the sun in the summer should bring it back again.' When she had finished the letter, the boy looked at her for a decision.

'Yes, you can go,' she said. 'But you'll have to stay the night. I'll not have you travelling that much in one day. Maybe your Aunt Letty would keep you.'

In the city they went to the Assembly Rooms and Danny passed his examination with the highest commendation. On the way down the steps, Miss Schwartz took his hand and although he made a slight attempt to take it away, she held tightly on to it. Then without looking at him, staring straight ahead into the rush hour traffic, she said,

'It's *not* too late. You can be great. If you try you can be really great.' She squeezed his hand so hard it hurt. Then she let it go.

'Did you say that to me?' asked Danny.

'Yes, Danny. To you.'

Afterwards they met a friend of Miss Schwartz's and went for tea in The Cottar's Kitchen. Danny had never seen her in such a joyful mood. She laughed and talked and praised him so much that he became embarrassed. She called him '*mein Lieber*' and introduced him to her friend as her star pupil, her *Wunderkind*.

'. . . and this is Mr Wyroslaski. He plays the cello in a symphony orchestra.'

He was a tall man with a very thin face. He had dark brown eyes, deep eyes, not unlike Miss Schwartz's own. His hair was very long, almost like a woman's.

'Why do all music people have funny names?' Danny asked.

'Like what?' asked Miss Schwartz.

'Like Schwartz and Wyro. . . Wyro — your name,' he said, nodding at her friend, 'and all those composers.'

'Names do not matter; you, *mein Lieber*, will be a great musician one day.'

'My name is Danny McErlane,' and the way he said it made them all laugh. Miss Schwartz leaned across the table and smacked a kiss off Danny's forehead. He blushed and looked down at his plate.

'Besides,' said Mr Wyroslaski, 'there is John Field. He is an Irish composer. Names do not matter. What matters is the heart, the mind. Did you ever hear of a composer called Joe Green?'

Danny nodded that he hadn't.

'That is English for Giuseppe Verdi.'

'Who's he?' asked Danny. He joined uncertainly in the laughter his question had started. Mr Wyroslaski looked at him and produced a large handkerchief from his pocket. He slowly folded it into a pad which he licked and leaned over to Danny.

'Marysia, you leave your mark on everyone.' He rubbed Danny's forehead hard. It surprised Danny that Miss Schwartz had a first name. He sounded it over in his mind, Maur-ish-a, Maur-ish-a. He never imagined himself calling her anything but Miss Schwartz.

Today she looked different. When she had come out of the Ladies' Room her black hair was down, falling over her shoulders. Her normally sallow cheekbones were pink and her eyes seemed to sparkle and flash more than they did in the darkness of her sitting room at home. She wore a brown suit and a blouse of creamy lace. At her throat was a cameo brooch which matched the brown of her suit. It was the first time Danny had seen her legs, the first time he had seen her out of her dressing-gown.

Danny had begun to dislike Mr Wyroslaski. He had pulled away from the handkerchief but the man's bony hand had held the back of his neck so that he couldn't. Now as Wyroslaski listened to Miss Schwartz his mouth hung open and his eyebrows were raised like pause markings, as if he did not believe what she was saying. His face was prepared for laughter even though nothing funny was being said. They were talking too much. Danny began reading the stained menu. Then Wyroslaski lowered one eyebrow and said something in a foreign language at which Miss Schwartz laughed, covering her lower face with both hands. She replied to him in the same sort of language. Danny turned the menu over but there was nothing on the back of it.

Eventually she turned to Danny and said,

'He is such a handsome boy, my archangel, isn't he? *Mein Lieber*, we all must go. Your Aunt Letty will be worried about you. Mr Wyroslaski has kindly said that he will drive you there in his car. What do you say?'

'Thank you,' said Danny.

'We'll drop you off and I'll see you in good time for the bus in the morning.'

As they rose from the table, Mr Wyroslaski flicked his hair out from his collar with his knuckled cellist's hand.

The next day on the long bus journey home, Miss Schwartz was quiet and often seemed not to be interested in or understand what Danny said to her. She did point out the freshness and greenness of everything. Hedges flashed by, fields moved, mountains turned in the distance.

'It is spring. The sap is rising, quickening in all things. Do you not feel it?'

'No,' said Danny. And they lapsed into silence again.

At the next lesson, Miss Schwartz opened the door in her familiar black dressing-gown.

'Well, Danny, have you forgiven me?'

'What for?'

'I thought you had fallen out with me. Is that not so?'

'No.'

'You did not feel neglected?'

Danny began searching through his pages for his piece. He shrugged.

'It was *your* day, Danny. It was wrong of me to enjoy it.'

He set his music on the piano.

'What did you think of Mr Wyroslaski? Wasn't he. . .'

'He smiled too much,' Danny interrupted her.

'You *are* annoyed, aren't you, Danny?'

'No.'

And she touched his hair with her extended hand and her faced opened in a warm smile of disbelief and delight.

After he played for her she asked,

'How did your mother like your certificate?'

'She says she's going to get Dad to frame it.'

'Tell her not to bother. There will be more. Bigger and better ones. And what's more, you can tell her I will give

93

you extra lessons and it doesn't matter whether she can pay or not. Two a week for the price of one. How would you like that?'

Danny was not so sure, but he said yes to please her.

In July Danny's sister married. The remainder of the guests from the hotel all crowded into the McErlanes' front room after the reception. Danny's mother sat stunned and a little drunk. Her husband, Harry, was even more drunk, but had through practice learned to keep going. He was asking everybody what they would have to drink. Aunt Letty, who didn't drink, was helping him pour the whiskeys and uncork the stout. Danny sat in the corner with an orange juice in his hand which he dared not drink. Everybody that day had bought him an orange juice.

'Well, that's that,' said Harry, falling back into an armchair, his knees still bent. He waved his thumb in the direction of the corner. 'There's only one left. The shakings of the bag has yet to go.'

'It'll be a while yet, Harry,' said a neighbour, 'and he'll only go when the notion takes him. He'll not be forced.'

Harry blinked his eyes and focused on whoever had spoken. It was Red Tam.

'Tam, I hope you're not meaning anything by that remark.'

'What do you mean "meaning"?'

'About being forced. There was no forcing at today's match and well you know it.'

'The child, Harry,' warned Mrs McErlane.

'My girl is a good girl. She'd have none of that sort of filth.' Danny's father spat the last word out.

'Aye, I know. Time will tell,' said Red Tam.

'What the bloody hell do you mean, "time will tell"? If it's a fight you want, Red Tam, we'll settle it right now.' He struggled to escape from the armchair. Red Tam put up his hands and laughed.

'I'm saying, Harry, that time will prove you right. That's all. You're too jumpy, man.'

Harry was not so sure. Mrs McErlane interrupted.

'Danny is going to play the piano for us. Won't you, son? A bit of entertainment will settle us all.'

'The old Joanna,' someone shouted above the din.

'Good stuff.' A spatter of applause went round the room. Danny blushed.

'I'd wash my hands of any girl that would allow herself to be led into that sort of dirt before marriage.'

'It happens, Harry. It happens.'

'Not in my house it doesn't.'

'Look at big Maureen from Bank Street. Thirty-two years old, they say. At her age you'd think she'd have known better.'

'An animal,' said Harry, 'if ever there was one. There was that many of them she didn't know who to blame. The beasts of the field. . .'

'Stop it, Harry. The child,' hissed Mrs McErlane. 'Go and get your music, son.' She turned in explanation to her neighbour, saying, 'He's not allowed to play without it.'

Danny lurched shyly from the corner, saying that he wouldn't, but hands grabbed him and guided him through the crowded room to the piano. He took out the music for the piece he had just been practising.

'What are you going to give us?'

Danny propped the music up, opened the lid and the room became silent, except for the noise of somebody in the kitchen washing dishes. He began to play a movement from a Haydn sonata.

'That's grand stuff,' said his father proudly through the music.

'Very highfalutin' but good. It's well done,' said Red Tam.

'He has the touch,' said Mrs McErlane. 'So his music teacher tells me. Miss Schwartz, y'know. But you'd know to listen to him yourself.'

Danny played on, the glittering phrases mounting in elegance. Letty leaned in from the kitchen and, aware that she had to be quiet, hissed,

'Harry, will you have another stout?'

'I will, aye.'

'Whisht till we hear,' said Danny's mother. Red Tam rang notes on his empty whiskey glass with a horny fingernail and waved it at Letty. The piece came to an end and Danny's fingers had barely left the keys but they were folding away his music. Everyone applauded loudly.

'What was that?' asked Red Tam.

'Haydn,' said Danny his voice barely audible.

'Grand. Do you know any Winifred Atwell tunes? Now there *is* a pianist. How she does it I just do not know. The woman must have ten fingers on each hand. Do you know "The Black and White Rag" at all?' Red Tam took a gulp of his new whiskey. 'Did you ever hear of her, Harry?'

'Aye, she's on the wireless, isn't she?'

'You can say that again. She's never off it. The money that woman must be making.' He shook his head in disbelief. 'And her coloured, too.'

'Do you like the rock and roll, Tam?' said Mrs McErlane, winking, 'I thought it would be right up your street.'

'Indeed I do not.'

'You're right there,' Danny's father joined in, 'I can't take this classic stuff the boy is at all the time but I know for sure the rock and roll is rubbish.'

'I like *some* classic stuff,' said Tam 'Mantovani. . .'

'I like good music — something with a bit of a tune to it,' Harry went on, 'Bing's my man.' He stuck the pipe in the corner of his mouth, his eyes closed, and he began to croon, slurring the words in an American accent,

'A'm dream-ing of a wha-ite Christmas.'

'Aye,' said Tam, interrupting the song, 'that's where the money is at. This rock and roll will not last.'

'It'll not be heard of in another year's time,' agreed Harry. 'The boy there could be making money before long. There's many's the dance band would snap him up if he was older. The classical stuff is all right. It gets the hands going. Good practice, y'know. But the bands is the place where the money is.'

'Or on the wireless,' added Tam. Harry rose and stood expansive and swaying in front of the fire.

'You did well at the speaking, Harry, for one that's not used to it,' said his wife.

'Aye. At least I kept it clean. Whis is more than I can say for some.'

'Uncle Bob. Wasn't that a disgrace.'

One of the others, drunker than the rest, overheard and mimicked,

'"The bride and groom have just gone upstairs to get their things together."' Half the people laughed again at the joke, Harry said,

'That man Bob has a mind like a sewer.'

Danny threaded his way to the door and once upstairs threw what was left of his orange down the lavatory.

They worked hard all through that summer, the boy in shirtsleeves at the piano, Miss Schwartz, despite the heat, still in her silk dressing-gown. One day Danny discovered that she wore nothing beneath it because when she bent over to point out some complexity in the score the overlap of her gown rumpled and he saw cradled there the white pear shape of one of her breasts. He pretended not to understand the notation but when she bent over again her dressing-gown was in order.

'The black marks, Danny. Pay attention to the black marks.'

He felt his knees shaky and could not concentrate to play any more.

After the lesson they would go out to the small garden and have tea beneath the apple tree, tea with no milk but a slice of lemon in it — a thing Danny had never heard of. Miss Schwartz had pointed out to him when the flowers had fallen off the tree and each week they inspected the swelling fruit. Lying back in striped deck chairs they both watched the flickering blue of the sky as it dodged between the leaves.

Miss Schwartz had resurrected from the attic an ancient wind-up gramophone on which she played records outdoors. Danny came to know many pieces. Sometimes if there was a concert on the wireless she would open the kitchen window, turn the volume up full and point the set towards the garden. One day, during a performance of Mahler's 'Kindertotenlieder', she said,

'You know, Danny, the reason I bought this house was because of the garden. We had one just like it when

I was a girl. I was about your age when we had to leave it.'

'Where was it?'

'In Poland. A place called Praszka. I remember it as beautiful.'

'Why don't you go back?'

She laughed. 'Because I am too long away. The longer you are away the more you want to go back. And yet you realise the longer you are way the more impossible it is to return. The early monks had a phrase for it — what you suffer. If you died for God, that was simple. That was red martyrdom. If you left your country for God and lived in isolation, that was white martyrdom. To be an exile, to be cut off from your country is a terrible thing.' She smiled. 'I left, not for God, but for convenience. It was a time of fear.' She shuddered and looked up into the apple tree.

Danny sat stripped except for his shorts. He glanced up to where the music was coming from and saw himself reflected brightly in the window. His hair had grown longer and darker. Light from a spoon on the tray lying on the grass reflected into his face.

'But it is not so bad. There are compensations,' she said, smiling at him.

Many times on his way home Danny would stop off at the forge, if it was open, and listen to the blacksmith. He loved the way the man did not shave often and had black bristles on his chin like the baddies in cowboy comics. He was always joking and talking. 'Am I right or am I wrong?' was his favourite phrase. One day, sitting astride his anvil, he talked about Miss Schwartz.

'She's a rum bird, isn't she?'

Danny nodded.

'Why do you agree with me? The nod of the head is the first sign of a yes-man. Well, are you just a yes-man?'

'No', said Danny and laughed.

'This bloody country is full of yes-men and the most of them's working class.' He dismounted from the anvil and began to rake the fire to life. 'Yes, your honour, no, your honour. Dukes and bloody linen lords squeezing us for everything we've got, setting one side against the other. Divide and conquer. It's an old ploy and the Fenians and Orangemen of this godforsaken country have fallen for it again.' He began to work the bellows himself and the centre of the fire reddened. Danny loved the colour of blue that the small flames took on when the fire was heating up. He could feel the warmth of the fire on the side of his face and his bare arm. The smith was now talking into the fire.

'But a change is coming, Danny Boy. We must be positive. Prepare the ground. Educate the people. Look to the future the way Connolly and Larkin did in 1913.'

He threw the poker down among the fire-irons with a clang and turned to Danny. His face changed and he smiled.

'You haven't a baldy notion what I'm talking about, have you?'

'No.'

'But am I right or am I wrong?'

'You're right,' was always Danny's answer.

It was about this time that Danny began to notice a change in Miss Schwartz. She became moody and did not smile or laugh as much as she used to. One day when he arrived early for his lesson, panting from running most of the mile, it was a long time before she opened the door. When she did she was thrusting a handkerchief up her sleeve and she had obviously been crying. Her eyes were heavy-lidded and red.

When she went in, she said, 'Get your breath back,' and began to water her plants from a small Japanese tea-pot, turning her back on him. She talked to the plants the way other people would talk to a pet. She said it encouraged them to grow.

'Lavish love and attention on growing things and they will not let you down.'

'What about your apple tree? Do you talk to it?'

'It hears music from the house.' She smiled weakly at her own answer.

'But I know houses . . .'

'Your piece, Danny. I want to hear it.'

Danny gave a small, knowing smile. Miss Schwartz half reclined on the sofa at the bay window, her feet gathered beneath her. She turned to face the light and waited. Danny set his music on the chair and began to play. It was the opening movement of the Beethoven C sharp minor Sonata. She disliked calling it, 'The Moonlight'. Danny looked round to see if she had noticed, but her eyes were closed. He played on, trying to feel the music as she would have felt it. Sunlight slanted into the room and Danny thought her face looked haggard. Some of her tight hair had come adrift and hung down by her throat.

When he finished Miss Schwartz opened her eyes and they were glassy with tears.

'How beautiful, Danny,' she said in a whisper.

'You didn't notice,' he said, his feet swinging on the stool.

'What?'

'I played it without the music.'

Miss Schwartz came to him.

'How utterly superb,' she said, taking his face in her hands. She put her arms around his head and gave him a tight squeeze of joy. Danny sensed the huge softness of her breasts against his cheek, enveloping his face, the faded scent of her, the goosefleshy wedge at her throat.

'Oh Danny, how superb.' This time she held him at arm's length, watching his blushes rise. Danny tried to dismiss it.

'I practiced it —

            all week end,' he said.

'Oh Danny,' Miss Schwartz let a gasp out of her. 'Say that again.'

'I prac —

             -tised it all week end.'

'Danny, your voice is breaking.' She put one hand over her mouth, a look of disbelief in her eyes. She sat down at the piano and asked him to sing some of the notes she played. His voice was accurate but kept flicking an octave down. She sat at the piano, her fingers poised above the keyboard, touching it but not heavily enough to depress the keys. Her head was bowed.

'The purest thing in the world is the voice of a body before it breaks,' she said, 'before he gets hair. Before he begins to think things — like that.' Her face looked the same way as when he played badly.

'But I hardly even notice it, Miss.'

'I do and that is sufficient,' she said. 'Today in the garden I will play you purity.'

The kitchen was full of a mute bustling as she made the tea. Danny carried the tray out, she the record. It was a boy soprano singing Latin. A blackbird from the ridge-tiles of the roof sang loud enough to drown certain passages. When the music was finished Danny said,

'My Mum says to tell you that I'm going to Grammar School.'

'You passed your Qualifying!' Danny nodded. 'Oh, I'm delighted. Which school?'

'Our Lady's High.'

'Hm.' She thought for a moment and then smiled. 'They don't have a music teacher as yet.'

Danny sat in the school yard eating his cheese piece, a bottle of milk in his hand. He saw Mingo coming across to him, his white hair weaving through the crowd. He had started the Grammar in September as well, but everybody knew that his father was paying for him.

'Hiya, piss face,' said Mingo. 'You still going out to that black bitch for music?' Danny looked at him but could not answer because the tacky cheese had stuck to the roof of his mouth.

'Sucker,' said Mingo. 'I don't have to go any more. Haw-haw-haw.' He spoke the laughter in words.

'Why not?'

'Because my old woman just stopped me. She was talking to Schwartzy in town and she came home and said, "That's it, no more music for you, my lad." Haw-haw-haw. McErlane the sucker still has to go.'

'It's O.K. She's not bad.'

'She has a good pair of tits on her,' said Mingo, groping the air before him. 'She likes you, McErlane. You're her pet. Does she ever let you feel her?' Danny looked at Mingo's flickering white eyelashes — he was constantly blinking behind his tinted glasses. He wanted to punch him in his foul mouth. Instead Danny said,

'I saw them one day.'

'Her tits?'

'Yeah.'

'What were they like?'

'Just ordinary.' Danny gestured with his hands.

'How did you see them?'

'She opened her dressing-gown one day and she wasn't wearing a . . . thingy.'

'Liar. I don't believe you.'

Danny shrugged and threw his crusts into the waste-basket.

'Were they nice bloopy ones?'

'Yeah.'

Danny sucked the bluish watery milk through a straw until it was finished. It made a hollow rattling sound at the bottom of the bottle. He asked Mingo,

'Are you going to music to anybody else?'

'There isn't anybody for miles, thank God.'

'I don't think I'd want to go to anybody else.'

'Aye, not if she shows you her tits, I don't blame you.'

There was a pause. Danny laced the used straw into a knot of angles.

'She shows them to more than you,' said Mingo.

'What do you mean?'

'She's a ride.'

'What's a ride?'

'Haw-haw-haw, he doesn't know.' Mingo folded up with mock laughter. 'She's going to have a baby.'

'So what?'

'So she's a ride.'

'How do you know?'

'My Mum says.'

'Your Mum's . . . a ride,' said Danny.

Mingo suddenly reached out and grabbed Danny by the ear, digging his nails into it shouting,

'Nobody says that about my Mum.'

Danny yelled out in pain and punched. He struck Mingo on the nose and dislodged his glasses. Mingo let go of Danny's ear and turned and ran, clutching his glasses to his chest, a trickle of blood on his white upper lip. He stopped at the far side of the playground and made a large 'up ya' sign with two fingers. It began at the ground and ended above his head. He kept doing it, jumping up and down to exaggerate the gesture. Danny turned away in disgust and slotted the empty milk bottle into the crate.

The road to Miss Schwartz's place was ankle-deep in brown scuffling leaves. The apples on the tree had become ripe and she had given Danny one. He bit into it and a section of its white flesh came away with a crack. Juice wet his chin.

'It must be the music,' he said crunching.

Now he practised with real determination, getting up with his father and doing an hour before school. He had to wait until his father went out because he said he couldn't stand the racket first thing in the morning. He did another hour in the evening before his father came in. His mother didn't seem to mind. She slept through the morning session and she would be out in the kitchen making Harry's dinner for most of the evening practice. She was glad to see the piano used so much. One evening Danny's mother came in to lay the table and stood watching him play.

'Your hair is getting darker. I thought the sun would have helped,' she said. Danny stopped playing.

'Mum,' he said, 'Miss Schwartz wants to know if you could pay her in advance for this term.'

'Oh, I don't think so. Look at the money I had to lay out for your uniform for the High.' She went to the cupboard and looked in the jar on the top shelf.

'No, tell her I'm sorry but I just can't do it.'

'A whole lot of her pupils are leaving.'

'Why's that?'

'I don't know,' said Danny, closing the lid of the piano.

It was shortly after this that the biscuits stopped. Miss Schwartz apologised and said that she was getting too fat. However, they still had tea together.

Danny's father, being a bus driver, got the pick of all the papers left in his bus, but the only one he would bring home was the *Daily Express*. He had a great admiration for it.

'First with everything,' he said, 'and no dirt.'

From his armchair he read a piece to Danny that said that the Russians had launched a satellite into space and

103

that it would be possible to see it for the next few evenings if conditions were right.

'It's wonderful too,' he said nodding his head. 'At one end of the world the Russians is firing things into outer space and we still have a blacksmith in the town shoeing horses.'

'He says he knows you,' said Danny.

'Who?'

'The blacksmith.'

'When were you talking to him?' His father's voice had risen in pitch.

Danny shrugged.

'After music,' he said.

'Well, you'll just stop it. You hear me? If I catch you in that forge I'll take my belt off to you.'

The loud voice brought Danny's mother out from the kitchen. Her head was cocked to one side with curiosity and concern.

'Who's this?' she asked.

'You know who — the blacksmith. If he's pouring the same poison into your ear, son, as he's been spewing out in the pub, he's a bad influence. He'd have you into guns and God knows what. Denying religion at the top of his voice.'

'God forgive him,' said Mrs McErlane.

'Aye, and what's more he said they weren't serious in 1922 because they didn't shoot a single priest.'

'Did he say that?'

'Do you hear me, Danny, steer clear of vermin like that or you'll feel the weight of my hand.'

The next lesson Danny told Miss Schwartz of the satellite. She agreed that they should go out at six and try to see it.

The night was cold, black and clear as a diamond. A swirl of stars covered the sky so that it seemed impossible to put a finger between two of them. And they stood and waited, their necks craned.

'Isn't it marvellous,' Miss Schwartz said. Danny said nothing. His eye was searching for the satellite.

'Can you see it?' he asked.

When they stopped walking, the crackling underfoot ceased and the silence seemed enormous. In the frost nothing moved. Then Miss Schwartz whispered,

'Look. Look there.' It was as if she had seen an animal and to speak would frighten it.

'Where?'

'Follow my finger.'

In the darkness Danny had to get close to look along the line of her arm. He smelt her perfume and the slightest taint of her own smell, felt his face brush the texture of her clothing.

'There,' she said, 'can you see it? Like a moving star. A little brighter than the rest.'

'Oh yes. I can see it now.'

They stood in silence, close to each other, watching the pin-point of light threading its way up the sky from the horizon. To their left was the faint orange dome of light from the town. When the satellite was directly above them it paused, or seemed to pause, and they held their breath, their faces dished to the sky. Miss Schwartz put her hand round Danny's shoulder.

'How utterly lonely,' she said. 'The immensity of it frightens me.'

They were silent for a long time, watching its descent down the other side of the sky, moving yet hardly moving. Some miles away a dog barked. A car's headlights fanned into the sky and they heard its engine as soft as breathing. Miss Schwartz said in a whisper,

'The music of the spheres. Do you hear it, Danny?'

'No. What is it?'

'It's a sort of silence,' she said and in the darkness he knew that she was smiling. Suddenly she returned to her normal voice.

'What I don't understand, Danny,' her fingers began to knead his shoulder, 'is how it stays up there. I'm very silly about these things. Why does it not fall down?'

'It's kind of suspended. Outside earth's gravity. I think the moon pulls it one way and the earth pulls the other and nobody wins — so it just stays up there. Something like that anyway. The papers say it will fall back to earth after a few months.

'Caught between the heavens and the earth. How knowledgeable you are, Danny.'

'The science teacher told us today at school.' He began to tremble with the cold.

'Oh, but you are shivering. We must go in or your mother will be angry with me. If you catch a chill she will have my life.'

Inside Miss Schwartz made tea while Danny waited, sitting on his stool by the fire, listening to a record he had chosen himself.

'I'm glad that you picked that one,' she said when she came into the room. 'On Sunday at church I will play you your favourite.'

'Which?'

'The Bach. "*Liebster Jesu, wir sind hier*".'

'What does that mean?'

'"Jesus we are here".'

'Seems a funny thing to say. You'd think he'd know that.'

'Sometimes I wonder,' she said, approaching her tea with her mouth because it was so hot without milk or a slice of lemon.

On his way home Danny followed the wobbling yellow disc his torch made on the ground. He was not afraid of the dark but felt protected by it in some way. He noticed from a distance that light was coming from the forge. The door was open and a slice of the roadway in front of it visible. The blacksmith must have heard him because when Danny stopped outside he began to sing 'Oh Danny Boy'.

'Come in,' he shouted. From the threshold Danny refused.

'Why not?'

'My Dad says I'm not allowed.'

The blacksmith laughed and said that he had a fair idea why.

'What would he do if he caught you here?'

'Take his belt off to me.'

The man snorted and came to Danny in the doorway. He rucked up his leather apron and thrust his hands into his pockets.

'Danny,' he said and there was a long pause. 'You're coming to an age now when you've got to think. Don't accept what people tell you — even your father. Especially your father. And that includes me.'

Danny eased his hip on to a large tractor tyre propped by the door.

'Your Dad and I have very different views of things. He accepts the mess the world is in whereas I don't. We've got to change it — by force if necessary.'

'Did you see the satellite?' asked Danny. The blacksmith nodded and laughed.

'It takes the Russians. I bet the Yanks feel sickened. That's an example of what I'm talking about. Equal shares and equal opportunity leads to progress, Danny. The classless society. It'll happen in Ireland before long. There's nothing surer. Am I right or am I wrong?'

Danny smiled and said that he would have to go. The blacksmith touched him on the shoulder.

'If you want to come back here, Danny, you come. The belt shouldn't stop you. You've got to be your own man, Danny boy.'

'I'll maybe see you.'

On the road Danny waited for the hammer blows so that he could walk in step but none came and he had to choose his own rhythm.

On Sunday Danny waited to hear the familiar thumping sound of Miss Schwartz taking her place in the organ loft. She was not the same religion as the McErlanes but she had told Danny that she had needed the money and that it was a chance to play regularly on the best organ for a radius of twenty miles. After mass she had taken him up several times into the loft and he had been astonished by the sense of vibration, the wheezes and puffs and clanks of the machinery which he hadn't heard from the church. He loved the power of the instrument when she opened the stops fully to clear the church.

He heard the door of the organ loft close and was surprised when he looked round to see a man. He was bald with a horseshoe of white hair and horn-rimmed spectacles. Throughout the distribution of communion he played traditional hymns with a thumping left hand and a scatter of wrong notes. Afterwards he drove away in a white Morris Minor.

Outside on the driveway Father O'Neill talked to Danny's mother. The boy was sent on ahead while they talked. All that Sunday the house was full of whispers. Danny would come into a room and the conversation would stop. He thought Miss Schwartz must be ill.

The next day, the Monday before Christmas, when he came home from school his mother was sitting at the table writing a letter. He gathered his music and was about to go out when she called him.

'Here's a note for your music teacher.' Then she added, 'Don't be too disappointed, son.'

'What do you mean?'

'Never mind. Just you take that to your teacher and maybe she'll explain.'

On the road the wind was cold. Some hailstones had fallen and gathered into seams along the side of the road. The wind hurt the lobes of his ears and the tip of his nose.

He gave Miss Schwartz the note and she opened it jaggedly with a finger. She chinked the money into her hand, then read the letter. She looked as if she was going to cry but she stopped herself by biting her lip. Her teeth were nice and straight and white.

'Play for me,' she said.

Danny began to play the Field Nocturne he had been practising. The dark descended slowly. When he had finished she said,

'Let us not have a lesson. Let us play all the best things.'

'You didn't play the organ on Sunday. Were you sick?'

'Yes. I was indisposed.' She thought for a while, then put her hand to the back of her head and untied her hair. With a shake she let it fall darkly forward.

'I'm pregnant,' she said. Danny nodded.

'That means I'm going to have a baby.'

'Yes, I know.'

'They don't want me any more.'

108

'Why not? You're the best organist I've ever heard.'

'You can't have heard many. No more talk, Danny. That's enough. What are you going to play?'

'Can I have the light on?'

'No,' she said. 'Play me the Schubert. You know it well enough to play in the dark. It makes the other senses better. In the dark we are all ears, are we not?' Her voice sounded wet, as if she had been crying.

'Which one?'

'The G flat.'

Danny began to play. Somehow he felt a sense of occasion, as if she was willing him to play better than he had ever played before. To feel, as she had so often urged him, the heart and soul of what Schubert had heard when he wrote down the music. In the dark he was aware of her slight swaying as he played. Now she sat forward on the sofa, her long hair hanging like curtains on each side of the pale patch of her face. She sat like a man, her knees wide apart, her elbows resting on them. The melody, more sombre than he had played it before, flowed out over the rippling left hand. Then came the heavy base like a dross, holding the piece to earth. The right hand moved easily into the melody again, the highest note seeming never to reach high enough, pinioned by a ceiling Schubert had set on it. Like the black notes he had struck in Uncle George's room by himself creating a disturbing ache. The piece reached its full development and swung into its lovely main melody for the last time. It ended quietly, dying into a hush. Both were silent, afraid to break the spell that had come with the music. Danny heard Miss Schwartz give a sigh, a long shuddering exhalation and he too sighed. She leaned forward and switched on a small orange lamp which stood on the side table.

'Danny, you are my last pupil. They have taken all the others away from me. But I do not care about them. They are money. But you are the best. You are more than that. You are the best thing I have ever had and when they try to take you away from me. . .' She stopped and dipped her face into the handkerchief she had rolled in her hand. She looked up at him and began again.

'This is your last lesson. Your mother does not allow you to come here again.'

'Why not?' Danny's voice was high and angry. Miss Schwartz raised her shoulders and splayed out her hands.

'I think in our time together we have accomplished much, Danny. There is so much more technique that you have to learn. But your heart must be right. Without it technique is useless. Sometimes I am ungenerous and doubt others' sensitivity. It is hard to believe that someone can feel as deeply as oneself. It is difficult not to think of oneself as the centre of the universe. But I believe in yours, Danny. I see it in your eyes, in your face. Do you know what a frisson is?'

'No.'

'It is a feeling that you get. Indescribable. A shivering. Your hair stands on end when you hear or read or know something that is exceptionally beautiful. Did you ever get that?'

'No.'

'Have you ever cried listening to a piece of music — not from sadness but from the sheer beauty of it? Have you ever *felt* like crying?'

'No. I don't think I have.' Danny wanted to please her but she asked the question with such a seriousness, beseeched him, that to tell a lie would have been wrong.

'I can only compare it to something which you have not yet experienced. Something you would not understand. But it will come. I'm sure it will come. That is what is wrong with this world. People are like the beasts of the field. They know nothing of music or tenderness. Anyone whom music has spoken to — really spoken to — must be gentle, must be kind — could not be guilty of a cruelty.'

She stood up and was walking back and forth with her fists tight.

'*Mein Lieber*, in the light the pale people see nothing. The glare blinds them. It is easy to hurt what you cannot see. To drop bombs a million miles away.' She stopped walking and pointed her finger straight at him. 'One of your Popes had a great thing to say once. He had been listening to some music by Palestrina with Palestrina himself. He said to him, "The law, my dear Palestrina, ought to employ your

110

music to lead hardened criminals to repentance." Do you think this,' and she hissed out the s sound, 'this town would do this to me if they had truly heard one bar of Palestrina? Listen. Listen to this.'

She stamped across the room and took out one of the books of records. She put one on and turned the volume up full and announced,

'Palestrina.'

She sat down on the sofa, rigid with anger, electricity almost sparking from her hair.

'Close your eyes,' she commanded.

Danny closed his eyes and let his hands rest on his bare knees. The unaccompanied singing seemed to infuse the room with sanctity. The clear male voices, intricate and contrapuntal, became an abstraction. Stairs of sound ascending and yet descending at the same instant. Danny thought of what she had said, her tirade. He thought of being taken away from this room, never to be allowed back again to talk and work with Miss Schwartz. Never to be allowed to call in on the blacksmith and be talked to as if he were a man. The garden, the sunlight, the tea. Her concern for everything he did and said. The pumping of the bellows and smell of coke. Her perfume and her laugh, her plants, her music. Her bare breast. Am I right or am I wrong, *mein Lieber*? He thought of being deprived of all this, never to be allowed back to it. And he began silently in his own dark to cry.

Miss Schwartz saw the tears squeeze from his eyes and she jumped from the sofa, all her anger gone, and rushed to him. In her haste the tail of her dressing-gown caught a pot-plant and it tumbled to the floor. Black loam spilled out and the dislodged plant fell from the pot, displaying its tangled skirt of white roots. She knelt before him, her arms about his waist. She too was crying. She kissed his knees and he felt her long hair tickle his legs as she swung her head back and forth.

'You are one of us, my love.'

She continued to weep, the tears streaming down her face, wetting her chin. It was only now that Danny felt her fatness through her gown, not soft fatness, but a hard pumped-up bigness pressing against him. She held him so tightly, so closely that after a time he was unsure whether the hardness belonged to him or to her. To stop himself falling off the stool he put his hands around her neck and as she pressed her cheek to his he felt the sliding wetness of it. She smelled beautiful in the darkness of her hair. She began to move in time to the music, crushing his face to hers. He heard and felt her mouth implode small kisses on the side of his face, moving towards his mouth, but he wrenched his head to the side, not knowing what to do. They stayed like that until the record ended with a hiss and the tick-tick-tick of the over-run.

Miss Schwartz got up from her knees and straightened her dressing-gown. She pushed back her hair and sniffed loudly.

'Go, Danny. Now. At once.'

He stopped at the door, his hand on the handle. She was kneeling again, sweeping the springy black loam with her hands into a pile on the mat. She knelt on her gown so that it pulled taut over the hump of her stomach and for the first time Danny saw how big it was. Her hands, dirtied with the soil, hung useless from her wrists.

'Promise me one thing before yo go,' she said. 'Find a good teacher. *Bitte, mein Lieber*. You might yet be great. Please — for me?'

Danny, unable to find the right words, nodded and left. Running in the swirling snow, the only thing he could think of was that she had not given him tea.

When he got home there was the worst row ever. Danny screamed and shouted at his mother, hardly knowing what he was saying. The answers they gave him he could not understand. They called her a slut and spoke of marriage and sin and Our Blessed Lady. He asked to be allowed back, he cried and pleaded, but his father ended it by thrashing him with his belt and threatening to take an axe to the piano.

Danny ran out into the night, down the garden, where he had built himself a hut of black tarred boards.

'Let him go, let him go,' he heard his mother scream.

The snow had lain and was thick under foot. The fields stretched white away from the white garden. Danny crawled into the darkness of his hut and squatted on the floor. He put his arms around his ankles and rested his wet cheek on his knees. He did not know how many hours it was he stayed like that.

He heard his mother coming out, her feet crunching and squeaking on the frozen snow.

'Danny,' she called, 'Danny.' She bowed down into the hut and took him by the arm. He had lost his will and when she drew him out, he came. The boy walked as if palsied, stiff and angular with the cold, his mother supporting him beneath his arm. He was numb, past the shivering point.

'Come into the heat, love,' she said, 'come in from the night. Join us.'

Heinemann
New Windmills

Alan Gibbons Chicken
Graham Greene The Third Man and The Fallen Idol; Brighton Rock
Thomas Hardy The Withered Arm and Other Wessex Tales
L P Hartley The Go-Between
Ernest Hemmingway The Old Man and the Sea; A Farewell to Arms
Nigel Hinton Getting Free; Buddy; Buddy's Song
Anne Holm I Am David
Janni Howker Badger on the Barge; Isaac Campion; Martin Farrell
Jennifer Johnston Shadows on Our Skin
Toeckey Jones Go Well, Stay Well
Geraldine Kaye Comfort Herself; A Breath of Fresh Air
Clive King Me and My Million
Dick King-Smith The Sheep-Pig
Daniel Keyes Flowers for Algernon
Elizabeth Laird Red Sky in the Morning; Kiss the Dust
D H Lawrence The Fox and The Virgin and the Gypsy;
Selected Tales
Harper Lee To Kill a Mockingbird
Ursula Le Guin A Wizard of Earthsea
Julius Lester Basketball Game
C Day Lewis The Otterbury Incident
David Line Run for Your Life
Joan Lingard Across the Barricades; Into Exile; The Clearance;
The File on Fraulein Berg
Robin Lister The Odyssey
Penelope Lively The Ghost of Thomas Kempe
Jack London The Call of the Wild; White Fang
Bernard Mac Laverty Cal; The Best of Bernard Mac Laverty
Margaret Mahy The Haunting
Jan Mark Do You Read Me? (Eight Short Stories)
James Vance Marshall Walkabout
W Somerset Maughan The Kite and Other Stories
Ian McEwan The Daydreamer; A Child in Time
Pat Moon The Spying Game
Michael Morpurgo Waiting for Anya; My Friend Walter;
The War of Jenkins' Ear
Bill Naughton The Goalkeeper's Revenge
New Windmill A Charles Dickens Selection
New Windmill Book of Classic Short Stories
New Windmill Book of Nineteenth Century Short Stories

How many have you read?